CW00495514

Parth

by
Adam Parish

Book 2 of the
Jack Edwards and Amanda Barratt
Mystery Series

Also by Adam Parish
The Quartermaster (1)
Loose Ends (3)

To sign up for offers, updates
and find out more about Adam Parish
visit our website www.adam-parish.com

This is a work of fiction. Names, characters, organisations, places, events and incidents are either products of the author's imagination or are used factually. Any resemblance to actual persons, living or dead is purely co-incidental.

ISBN 979-8-5988-2974-5

Thanks to Helen for her
help, humour, and patience,
and
Grace and Rachel
for their idea.

Chapter 1

The freshness of the falling rain did something to dissipate the rancid odours emitting from the black rubbish bags which littered the lane and were the temporary bedding of Ash Ashanti. Ash was twenty-eight years old, but already he was a man who had knowledge and experience of the finer things in life. His wealthy, aristocratic family could trace a line back about a thousand years. He had been to a Buckingham Palace garden party, had worn tails at Ascot, and felt nothing about dropping £10,000 on a single race. He had been up close, sometimes very close, with many London celebrities. Ash was, as they say, connected.

With a minor effort he opened his eyes, and with a bigger effort tried to move his prone body. Its response was not satisfactory, and he settled for an agonising movement of his arm the ten or so inches to a half-full bottle of whisky. With a further effort he raised the bottle at an angle which allowed him to fill his mouth. The whisky was cold and sharp but compelling enough to encourage him to go back for more, and he drank until almost all of it completed a painful journey to the pit of his empty stomach. The sensation surged through his system and forced him into a sort of consciousness.

This allowed him to contemplate the sticky remains of what might once have been a curry. It had probably been appetising once but, even to Ash's dull senses, that had obviously been some time ago, and now the rancid odour of the partly liquefied form – emerging from a rip in a bag near his right eye – induced a short period of uncontrolled retching. The retching was painful, but at least it told Ash that he was still alive, and with difficulty he put some distance between himself and the offending curry. This achieved, Ash felt that he might be able to stand up now, and a stretch of both legs confirmed this.

The drugs will not win, his inner voice thundered.

You'll never do it, another voice returned, while another, wearier, intonation questioned the point of it all.

The raindrops were large and wet as they burst onto his face. They were sweet and pure. He shut his eyes and enjoyed them.

The flash of a light and a gathering roar from a car broke the moment, and Ash was rudely roused as the vehicle sped down the single-track London lane. Its near-side wheels missed his feet by inches, and although injury was narrowly avoided, insult in the form of a deluge from a disturbed puddle followed rapidly and he spluttered.

He cursed the driver and raised himself just in time to see the red tail-light join the busy road and then, just as suddenly, all was quiet again. Ash looked down and lamented the state of his Armani suit. It was stained and torn: a perfect metaphor for himself and his current state.

He would make everything right – right with Jimmy and right with Laura. Jimmy had been about as good a friend as a man could ever ask for, and Ash, in a blinding moment of clarity, felt the weight of his own dependence on Jimmy's friendship. It was all very well saying he would make things right, but he didn't have a clue where to start. As for Laura … well, the jury was still out as to who had been right and who had been wrong, but Ash knew he would win her back.

There was no time like the present, and, after a few stumbling attempts, he gained the vertical and spent several moments dusting assorted detritus from his high-fashion garments. He then started a careful search of his pockets, which yielded a ten-pound note and a small packet of his favourite white powder.

In a moment of intense resolution, he raised his aching arm and propelled the drug into the black of the London night, where it settled behind some overflowing dustbins. He studied the ten-pound note carefully and decided that it might serve as a taxi fare, then took tentative steps towards the bright lights at the end of the lane.

Progress was slow, Ash having to stop and rebalance every few steps with occasional use of a back door as a means of support. About halfway out of the lane, he cursed his slow progress and persuaded himself that it would be no breach of his recent covenant if he returned to retrieve the whisky bottle. He made swifter progress back, and, after an undignified hunt among the rubbish bags, he located the bottle and took a last satisfying draught.

A break in the night clouds revealed that the bottle was now empty, so he threw it towards a dustbin. He missed. It shattered into many pieces with a deafening crash. Then everything was silent. For no reason, he decided the journey would be quicker the other way, and he set off, this time a little surer, in the opposite direction.

At first it seemed to be a bad decision for, as he walked, the distance to the end of the lane seemed further. The rain fell harder than ever, and the tunnel effect of the lane increased the wind's speed. Although it was summer, he couldn't stop his teeth chattering.

He stepped ankle deep into another puddle and cursed. The end of the lane seemed no nearer, and even the vague light from the main street ahead was no longer visible.

He grunted and focused his energy towards his legs and, at last, they responded. After a few steps, he gained enough confidence to look directly ahead. Screwing up his eyes, he became vaguely aware of why the light at the end of the lane was obscured.

At first the black silhouette seemed without form or motion, but as Ash's senses returned, he recognised beyond a doubt that another person was moving towards him.

The backstreets and alleys of London were home to a large population of assorted tramps and itinerants, and Ash's reduced circumstances of late had occasioned many such casual encounters. He pressed ahead towards the figure and, as they neared, Ash recognised the traditional dress code of a fellow unfortunate: a heavy coat and a half balaclava over the face.

Ash thought he might get in first and ask the other for a cigarette, but as he was constructing a form of words, his brain frantically issued another message. There was something wrong with the other guy. It was his gait – not shuffling and weak, but powerful and confident – that delivered this warning.

But the warning was too late. A thin steel blade slipped easily into Ash's neck, and bright red, heavy blood finally put paid to Ash's Armani suit.

Chapter 2

Amanda Barratt looked out of the window of her fifteenth-floor London office. The view was good and the office was large. Only one thing was missing: work. She was three months into a six-month secondment to the Home Office. It was a prestigious appointment, reserved for the highest of high fliers in the police and security services, a chance to meet with some of the most senior folks in the service: a box that needed to be ticked.

She was bored. There was nothing she could call her own. She wanted a case.

The phone rang and she answered it hopefully. It was a familiar voice. Baxter was her boss and he was near the top of the British security establishment. He had been allocated as her mentor. "How are you, Amanda?"

"Oh, so, so. It's very interesting seeing how other folks do it."

He laughed. "So, you're bored?"

She was forced to admit it.

"Well, I've got something for you. It might be nothing but I need a few enquiries made, discreetly. Just reporting to me."

She held the phone a little closer to her ear.

"There was a murder last night behind King's Cross Station," Baxter said. "On the surface it was just another mugging. The dead man is Ash Ashanti, a high-class car salesman in the West End. There's probably nothing in it, but he had a cheque on him. Fifty thousand pounds from the Samms Corporation."

"A lot of money," Amanda said. "Who are the Samms Corporation? I've never heard of them."

"Unsurprising. They are headed by a woman called Cora Samms. Have you heard of her?"

Amanda hadn't.

Baxter sounded wistful. "She's a bit of a legend. International woman of mystery. Origin unknown, art collector and as reclusive as Howard Hughes. Anyway, the Samms Corporation has grown and grown and is on our list."

"List? List of what?"

"A few companies are so secretive that, when their name comes up, there's an automatic referral to my department. We look into it and add any interesting information to our files. Just have a sniff around and see what turns up. It's an Inspector Bradley at Marylebone. Introduce yourself, but keep anything you find out about the Samms Corporation to yourself. Give me a ring if there's anything you need or I need to know."

"Okay, sir. I'll be in touch."

It wasn't much, but it was a job.

Chapter 3

At Marylebone, Inspector Bradley had a cold and Amanda got the impression he was enjoying it. He was surrounded by tissues, some well-used. When Amanda entered his office, he was popping a couple of aspirins. He blew his nose loudly and conducted a discreet review of the tissue's contents. He looked up, and in a hoarse voice said, "Oh, good morning, ma'am."

"Hi Danny," she said. "I won't ask how you are."

Bradley blew his nose again. "Damn summer colds. So, what brings you here? I thought you were flying high at the Home Office?"

She laughed. "Something like that."

He looked at her quizzically. "What can I do for you?"

"You've got a murder. At King's Cross."

He narrowed his eyes. "Just another mugging. Now why would that interest a big star like you? Of course – the cheque?"

She nodded. "It's a lot of money."

Bradley rose wearily, pulled a folder from a side cabinet and started leafing through it. "Ah, here it is." He held it aloft avariciously. "I could do with this," he said sadly and threw it to Amanda.

It was just a cheque, but it wasn't what Amanda had expected. It wasn't payable to Ash Ashanti. It was paid to self and signed by him. The account was titled Samms Corporation no. 29. This was nothing to do with car purchases. Ash Ashanti, car salesman, was a signatory on a Samms Corporation account. Interesting.

She didn't share this thought with Bradley. "What have you got?"

He sniffed, then sneezed and his whole body shook. "Not much. A stabbing at the back of the station. Not uncommon, unfortunately."

"DNA, blood, witnesses?"

"Nothing like that." Bradley spread his hands out in front of him. "It looks like one of those street bust-ups. That cheque was the only thing left. It was in his sock. They took everything else. The cheque was the only reason we know who he is. It seems he was well known about the West End – been warned about drugs once or twice. We managed to get hold of his business partner last night, Jimmy Trent. He came in and identified the body and gave us a few details. Ashanti lived alone, at a flat in the West End. An expensive flat."

"Have you been there yet?"

"Not yet."

"Friends, business associates, girlfriends?" Amanda asked.

"Give me a chance, ma'am!"

"When are you planning to go to the flat?"

Bradley sighed. "Well, it needs to be done today."

Amanda looked at him. "No time like the present."

Chapter 4

At a fashionable block of flats near Park Lane, Amanda, Bradley and Detective Constable Rose were engaged in a short discussion with an elderly concierge. He studied each of their warrant cards closely, was silent for a moment, and then finally allowed them the spare key to Ashanti's flat. In a further nod to security and privacy, he accompanied them to the second floor and insisted on personally admitting them.

Amanda held back a pace or two as they moved into a narrow hallway. Bradley and Rose went into the bedrooms and the kitchen, while Amanda drifted through to the main lounge diner. For a man in his twenties, the flat was a surprise. It could have been a show flat. The furnishings were expensive and tasteful and, on first sight, Amanda could detect none of the clutter that nearly every home accumulated.

In this room there were two facing sofas with an attractive-looking log burner between. It hadn't burnt logs for a long time. Above it, on the wall, was a large and arresting splash of colour. Amanda didn't know much about art but it suited the room. At the other end of the room a dining table was set for two people.

Nothing to learn here. She went through to the kitchen. There was nothing in the fridge and the bin was empty. She was about to declare it an information-free zone when she noticed a couple of cards pinned to a small corkboard. The first was a reminder of a doctor's appointment, and the second a business card for the Premier Car Company.

Bradley came in. "Nothing in the bedrooms except a lot of designer clothes."

DC Rose added, "Thousands of pounds' worth, ma'am – Armani, Calvin Klein, Burberry, that sort of thing."

Rose was no more than mid-twenties, good-looking, and, from the cut of his suit, a reliable authority on designer clothes.

"Was it you who identified Mr Ashanti last night?" Amanda asked.

He looked pleased with himself. "Yes, ma'am. I knew the name from the cheque. His car showroom is on my old patch. Quite a few of the guys in the station knew him."

"Good job." She turned back to Bradley and handed him the business and appointment cards.

"Yes, that's the company he worked for."

"Have we spoken to any of these?"

"Well, the garage is our next stop. You going to tag along?"

"Why not?" As an afterthought, she said, "What about the doctor?"

Bradley shrugged.

I'll go and see him and get a bit of background if you like?"

Bradley visibly perked up at that. "Okay."

She rang the number on the appointment card and arranged an appointment for eleven. The doctor was in.

Chapter 5

Bradley excused D.C. Rose, and, Amanda beside him, he pulled his unprepossessing police car into the car park of Prestige Cars and abandoned it between a Bentley and a Maserati.

There were a lot of other super-looking cars – Amanda supposed that's what they were called – sitting outside the main showroom. A teenager was lovingly cleaning one of them, and he looked up as they got out.

"Hello, can I help you?"

"We're looking for Mr Trent," Bradley said.

"In the showroom. His office is up the stairs."

The stairs were narrow, aluminium and dangerous.

On the mezzanine level there were two offices. A tall, good-looking man of about forty emerged from one of them. He extended his hand and, in a Scottish accent, said, "Good morning. Jimmy Trent, managing director. Come in."

The office was sparklingly clean and expensively furnished. Probably to make people feel good about parting with huge sums of money.

Bradley introduced himself and gestured to Amanda. "This is Amanda Barratt, a Home Office colleague." He took out a notebook, "Thanks for your help last night, Mr Trent. We just need a few more details. Mr Ashanti was a business partner?"

Trent stared down at his hands. "Yes, a full partner. We started it together."

"How did you meet?"

"I met him two or three years ago at a party. He was looking for something to do and so was I. He knew dozens of the London elite, or at least those with money. I knew about cars. It was an easy decision."

"Where did you learn about cars, Mr Trent?" Amanda asked.

"I was a captain in the Engineers, British Army."

"So how has the business been going?" Bradley asked.

Trent leant back in his chair. "Mostly really good. Ash has … had … so many contacts. He was a charming guy. Everyone liked him."

Amanda considered correcting him, but Trent got there first. "Well, I suppose not everyone."

"So was Mr Ashanti in here every day?" Bradley asked.

Trent laughed. "No, actually he wasn't in the office much at all. Well, he didn't need to be. He just needed to keep sending folks our way."

"You did all the day-to-day work?"

"Yes."

"Did you resent that, Mr Trent?"

Trent's eyebrows rose. "No, not at all, why should I? He was out and about every day. Where else would you get such a marketing and sales resource? Our arrangement was completely satisfactory. He did what he was good at, and so did I."

Bradley looked down at his notebook. "When did you last see him?"

"About a week ago," Trent said after a moment. "He popped in to give me the name of a prospect."

"How was he?"

Trent shrugged. "Much the same."

"I don't have all the details at the moment, but would it surprise you to learn Mr Ashanti was drunk and may have been taking drugs?"

Jimmy Trent laughed mirthlessly and shook his head. "No, Inspector, that wouldn't surprise me. Ash had a big appetite for things that weren't always good for him."

"Was that a problem for the business?" Amanda asked.

"Not really, it wasn't a nine-to-five job."

"Does Mr Ashanti have family?"

Trent shrugged. "Not that I knew. I never heard him talking about family."

"Where was he from?"

"Originally?"

"Yes."

"I really don't know. Middle East or somewhere like that. He never talked about that either."

Amanda tried again. "Girlfriend, boyfriend, anyone special?"

Trent laughed. "Plenty of girlfriends, but, well, never anything steady or for too long." He cocked his head a little. "Although recently … I can't be sure, but he made a few comments. Joking about settling down, that sort of thing. I think he mentioned a second date or something."

"And the name of this lucky lady?"

Trent shook his head. "Sorry, no idea."

"What vehicles did the Samms Corporation buy from you?" Amanda waited for his reaction.

"The Samms Corporation?" Trent asked blandly. "None, I've never heard of them."

"Do you need to check your records?"

"No, I know every car we sell. We're a low-volume, high-value operation."

"Did Mr Ashanti ever take deposits or payments for cars?"

Trent grimaced. "I preferred him not to. Generally, not. It was easier if we handled that at the office."

"Would you have any objection if we had a look in his office?" Bradley asked.

Trent stood up. "No, not at all. I doubt there's anything there.

Ash was hardly there and he was pathologically tidy. Do you want to see it now?"

The pair of them went out of the office. Amanda waited until she heard the second office door click open. She leant forward and pulled a sheet of paper from Trent's desk.

Nothing was as distinctive as a communication from Her Majesty's Customs and Excise. The typeface never varied, irrespective of the scale of the demand. This demand was six months overdue and it totalled, with fines, nearly £400,000.

She replaced the document just before Trent returned with Bradley.

"Nothing in the office," Bradley said.

Trent said, "Can you tell me a bit more about Ash's death? They didn't tell me much last night. Did anyone see it?"

"No, we have no witnesses so far. He was found down a back alley, near King's Cross. A restaurant employee found him when taking rubbish out the back door."

Trent's features tightened. "Not much of a way to go … Is there anything else you need at the moment?"

Amanda looked behind Trent to the numerous photographs on the wall. Mostly they were of delighted customers taking delivery of expensive shiny new cars. She pointed at one. "Is that Ash?"

He looked back and confirmed her suspicions.

"You got a spare one that I could have?"

Trent went into a desk drawer and drew out a full handful of photographs. "Take your pick."

She had a quick review and selected one. "Thanks. Where are you from, Mr Trent?"

He smiled. "Glasgow, but it's been a long time."

She returned the smile. "One of my best friends is from there. Talks about football a lot."

"Yes, that's Glasgow."

Amanda rose and Bradley did the same. Bradley said, "Oh, sorry, Mr Trent, just for our records, can you tell me where you were yesterday?"

If Trent was offended by the question, he didn't show it. "In the office until about six and then a quiet night in."

"Alone?"

"Sadly, yes. I was at home until I got your call."

Bradley put his notebook back in his pocket. "Thanks, Mr Trent. We might have to have another word."

He got up and walked with them. "No problem, let me know." He handed them both business cards, and escorted them safely down the precipitous staircase and out to their car. He brushed the paintwork of the police car. "If you are ever looking for a performance car …"

Amanda laughed, and as they drove off, she looked in her rear-view mirror and saw Trent watching them leave, a thoughtful look on his face. She had an awful feeling he had noticed that his papers had been disturbed.

Chapter 6

Just before eleven, Bradley dropped Amanda outside the doctor's surgery and headed back to the police station. They arranged to meet later and compare notes.

Amanda entered a small empty waiting room and crossed to the reception. "Amanda Barratt to see Doctor Hunt. I called earlier."

The blonde-haired girl looked around the room – unnecessarily, Amanda thought – and got up slowly. "This way."

She knocked on a door and a booming male voice responded, "Come."

The consulting room had once been modern and opulent but it looked tired now. So did the man behind the desk.

Dr Jasper Hunt firmly closed a battered folder on his equally battered desk and looked up. He indicated a seat and leant back in an unsteady-looking chair.

He shut his eyes, yawned, stretched several times, opened his eyes wide, and then groped around his desk until he located a pair of stylish but worn glasses.

He looked at Amanda through the dirty glasses and, after a moment of what appeared to be intense appraisal, smiled. Dr Jasper Hunt looked about sixty – but an old sixty. He pushed the folder along his desk to conceal what looked like a racing newspaper and said, "Miss Barratt, what can I do for you?"

"I'm from the Home Office and I'm investigating the death of a man called Ash Ashanti. I understand he was a patient of yours?"

"Yes, he was my patient." Hunt looked at the ceiling. "What happened – drugs?"

"No, Doctor, he was murdered."

Hunt's eyes widened a bit but he said nothing.

"How long was he a patient of yours?" Amanda asked.

Hunt had another folder on the desk, which he consulted. "Two years, Miss Barratt."

"And his medical history?"

"Not much, really. He was a young man, just twenty-eight years old." Hunt leafed through the pages. "He was here a bit more frequently recently, but just infections and things. Nothing serious."

"You mentioned drugs, Doctor Hunt?"

Hunt screwed up his wrinkled face. "Well, I suspected it, just in the last months. I asked him about it but he just laughed."

"Did he admit to drug use?"

"Oh yes. Said it was just social."

"And you believed that?"

Hunt sighed. "Miss Barratt, if I intervened with every young person who uses drugs, then … There's so many nowadays."

"When did you last see him?"

Hunt consulted his folder again. "Two months ago. Minor infection. I gave him some antibiotics."

"Did you know him before he was a patient?"

"No, of course not."

"And socially? I understand he was quite well known around the West End?"

"I believe he was a car salesman or something. Was always boasting about his cars and trying to sell me one."

"Did you buy one?"

Hunt laughed. "Of course not. The NHS doesn't pay that well." He looked at her hard.

Amanda tugged her black skirt down an inch nearer her knees.

"And there's nothing else you can tell me about him?"

"No, nothing, Miss Barratt. What happened to him?"

"We found him dead behind King's Cross Station. He had been attacked. Robbed and stabbed."

"Nasty," Hunt said after a moment.

Amanda had an afterthought. "Who is his next of kin?"

Hunt went into his file and extracted a sheet of paper, which he put in front of her. The relevant box was empty.

"Oh. I think that's all I need at the moment. Thanks for your time, Doctor Hunt."

He rose and stood very close to her while escorting her from his surgery.

The waiting room was still empty. On a whim, Amanda turned back to the receptionist. She flashed her the photograph.

The receptionist beamed. "That's Ash."

"You know him?"

"Of course, he was always in here."

Chapter 7

Amanda Barratt looked good from the back as well as the front. If only Hunt were twenty years younger. He couldn't do anything about that, though. He walked slowly out of his room and to the reception desk. "I need to go out, Sophie. I won't be back today."

She didn't look up but managed a low acknowledgement. There were no appointments anyway.

Returning to his room, an unknown joint cracked loudly. He stopped and caught sight of himself in a full-length mirror. His face alternated between a rugged sort of handsomeness of a sort and outright collapse. He ignored this unwelcome feedback and returned to his desk and reached for the racing paper.

In desultory fashion, he reviewed pages of advice before finally settling on a couple of lightly researched horses. He bet lavishly via one of his few online betting accounts still in credit.

He switched off his computer, picked up a packet of cigars and left without a word to his receptionist, emerging into the heat of the London afternoon.

A few paces brought him to his red two-seater. He dropped the soft top, and, to the accompaniment of Wagner's flying Valkyries, the car roared into life. The traffic was light and, taking advantage of a short gap, he red-lined the powerful vehicle.

Today, life was good.

Chapter 8

Before Amanda had decided whether to walk or to hail a taxi, her mobile rang; it was her boss, and the call was brief. She changed her route, and after a short walk sat down alongside him in a nondescript cafe.

Baxter was one of the UK's top spies but he looked like any other corporate executive. His shirt was open at the collar and his sleeves were slightly rolled up.

"Amanda, have a seat. You want a drink?"

"No thanks."

"How you getting on?"

"Not much so far," she admitted. "Just a rotten, everyday murder. Nothing out of the ordinary – except, of course, this cheque." She passed it across to him.

"Interesting. A relative or associate of Samms?"

"Could be. I'm looking."

"Anything else?"

"Not yet, sir."

He didn't appear disappointed. "It's not easy. Everyone's heard of her, but no one ever gets to meet her."

Amanda said, "Do you know anyone who has met this woman? Does she even exist?"

"Oh, she exists." He took a mouthful of coffee. "I met her once. About thirty years ago. I was about twenty and the lowest-grade private secretary at Downing Street. I was working the weekend and next thing the prime minister's standing alongside. She said, 'Only you here? Come with me – I've got a job for you.'"

Baxter's eyes took on a faraway look. "I followed her into the cabinet room. There was only one person there. A slim girl, about my own age." He smiled at the recollection. "I was told to sit down. It was weird. I thought maybe the girl was a relative or something."

Baxter wasn't one of those senior managers that specialised in boring those around him with stories of the old days. Amanda was riveted.

"I wasn't introduced. But the PM said, 'We need a short agreement typed up.' She gave me a few details, I typed it up, and they both signed. Then the PM said, 'Not a word about this, and no copies. Send the original to Sir Patrick.' He was the Cabinet Secretary then."

"And the girl was Samms?" Amanda asked.

"Yes, I found that out later."

"And the agreement?"

Baxter looked at her. "A fifty-year leasing arrangement for siting an army research facility on her land."

Amanda was about to ask more but Baxter cut her short.

"Anyway, I've got something else you might be interested in. I got a call yesterday from an old school friend, Colonel John Braid. Haven't seen him for years. He's a career soldier and he's currently running a very sensitive project. He's a decent guy, quite able but not all that ambitious. He was at Sandhurst with me. It'll probably be his last assignment before retirement."

It occurred to Amanda that Baxter himself was nearing retirement. She'd never really thought of that before.

"Braid's worried. He said he was calling me unofficially. Swore me to secrecy in fact." A smile passed across Baxter's face. "He's working with some pretty dangerous material and Braid tells me that he's worried about it."

"Why worried?" Amanda asked.

"He thinks some of it has been mislaid. He didn't tell me much more, but just asked my advice. I told him to re-check things and call me again if he needed to. John Braid's boss is a Colonel Shaw. He's based in Whitehall. Do you know him?"

Amanda shook her head.

"Surprised you haven't run into him. He's on the fast track like you. He's ticked all the right boxes, Blues and Royals, special forces, that sort of thing. He's a good politician as well. Word perfect on every progressive issue you can think of."

Amanda sighed; she knew the type.

"He's currently Head of Special Projects attached to the Royal Navy. His project is called Project 42. It's one of those projects so long-term that it's difficult to muck things up. He's about a year or so into a two-year secondment. There's really not a lot to do. Just sign off requisitions, read a few reports. Mostly he spends his time meeting faces in Whitehall. As for the project, it's a research programme. Bombs, I think."

Baxter gave her a hard look across the table. "It's not the sort of thing we want to go wrong. Braid's no genius, but he's a solid manager and he's loyal."

"Do you want me to talk to or go and see Braid?"

Baxter laughed. "No, not at the moment."

"Shaw?"

"Yes, why not?"

"You want me to talk to him about Braid?" This conversation was hard work.

"No, no, say nothing about Braid or about my conversation with him."

"What's my back story?"

Baxter shrugged. "Just talk to him about your murder and the cheque from the Samms Corporation. You are trying to tie up loose ends. Play it down."

What was all this about? She cocked her head in enquiry.

Baxter smiled at her. "As I mentioned, Braid's project is top secret and he handles very sensitive material. That's why he's based in the middle of the North Atlantic Ocean. On Cora Samms' island."

Chapter 9

Amanda introduced herself, and Colonel Shaw's secretary picked up a phone and made a call. She led Amanda into the large and uncluttered office of Colonel Shaw. A well-made man of about forty in a well-fitting suit rose from behind his desk and shook her hand.

"Mike Shaw," he said.

"Amanda Barratt, Home Office."

He indicated four high-backed chairs which surrounded a circular mahogany table and smiled pleasantly. "Nice to meet you, Miss Barratt. What can I help you with?"

Amanda flashed him a smile back. "Thanks for seeing me, Colonel Shaw. I'm investigating a murder, and, in the course of my enquiries, I've established a possible connection with the Samms Corporation."

Shaw's smile faded.

Amanda continued smiling. "It's been tricky to get information about this company, and I'm told that maybe you can help me."

Shaw looked at her. "Hardly. I am aware of them, as I expect you know, but I have no day-to-day dealings with them."

"None?"

"No. We just lease a bit of land, that's all. An island in the North Atlantic. A long-term lease."

She paused and stayed locked on him. "And Cora Samms?"

He scoffed. "No one has dealings with Miss Samms."

Amanda raised an eyebrow and waited for him to continue.

He sniffed and spread his hands. "Cora Samms is very low profile. Really, very few know much about her. I've heard people say she's a Sephardic Jew from Syria, others that she's a Shia Muslim from Iran, and some say she's from Eastern Europe. Who knows? She's about sixty years old, apparently, but that's all I know – or rather heard. Most of it might be rumours."

"What I do know," Shaw added, "is that she came onto the scene in the seventies or eighties. She purchased the Isles of Grace and transformed them. It was rumoured that she met Margaret Thatcher at the time of the Falklands War, and that led to an agreement for the construction of British facilities on the island."

"The Isles of Grace?" Amanda hadn't heard of it.

"Off the north west of Scotland."

"So, it's just us on the island."

"No, I understand Samms lives on the island. Actually, it consists of two separate islets." He screwed up his eyes. "One's called Main – that's where she lives – and the other's called Lessor, and that's where our base is."

"Just the place if you want to be a recluse. Anything else?"

"Apparently she has a collection of artworks rumoured to be worth billions. She is fanatical over art, they say. But her wealth and its origin, that's another mystery."

"So, you have no personal dealings with this mysterious lady?"

"None."

"If I wanted to meet her, who would I speak to?" Amanda asked.

Shaw raised his hand as if batting the idea away. "Impossible. You would have to go very high, Miss Barratt."

"Would you have objections to me attempting to contact Miss Samms?"

"Surely that is hardly necessary. What is it you are investigating?" Shaw looked serious. "Nothing to do with our base,

I hope?"

She took a long draught of coffee. "Last night, a down-and-out was found stabbed to death in a doorway near King's Cross."

She paused to gauge Shaw's reaction. He looked suitably incredulous, but didn't say anything.

"Seems he was once quite a minor celebrity in the London social scene. Ash Ashanti was his name. He was also a car dealer to the stars: premium marquees, Maseratis, Aston Martins – that sort of thing—"

"What on earth can the death of a car salesman have to do with Cora Samms?" Shaw snapped.

"Oh, probably nothing," Amanda said cheerfully, "but the car salesman … well, he wasn't always in such straitened circumstances."

"So what?"

"He was carrying a cheque drawn against the Samms Corporation. Given the Samms Corporation is a difficult corporate structure to penetrate, we could cut out a lot of unnecessary leg-work if we could talk to Miss Samms directly."

"Probably a payment for some of these cars," Shaw said dismissively. He puffed his chest out. "Look, Cora Samms is very wealthy, well connected and is a great friend of the British Government. She's reclusive and jealously guards her privacy. Because you are here, you must know" – he was getting angry now – "that she is, at present, providing us with invaluable services in relation to a top-secret military project."

His tone had switched to formal now. "I should add that the services that Miss Samms provides took many years to agree and negotiate. The arrangement is secret, sensitive, and any disruption could endanger the entire agreement. Therefore, we would strongly recommend, and indeed require, that there is no formal contact with Miss Samms."

Interesting.

He added, "Of course, if you have any simple, specific enquiries,

I may be able to intercede and establish whether someone in the corporation could shed any light on your enquiry."

Amanda nodded, but she wasn't going to hand over the assignment to Shaw who, by his own admission, would hardly pursue his enquiries vigorously. "We could, of course, just carry on," she said. "I mean we don't actually need your blessing. Of course, we are always keen to cooperate."

Shaw drummed his fingers on the desk. "Yes, we are always happy to cooperate. However, until you've got a more compelling reason, I must respectfully request that no contact is made with Miss Samms."

Amanda did not argue; instead, she asked a question which she knew he wouldn't answer. "What exactly are we doing on Cora Samms' island?"

"I can't discuss precise details, save to say that without her cooperation some very important military research and development would be impossible. She affords us the facility and the privacy to continue our research. I cannot say further."

Amanda clasped her hands together and rose with a smile. "Yes, that's fine. I'm sure these details are not likely to be needed. Thanks for your time, Colonel Shaw."

He accepted her handshake but didn't rise to escort her from his office.

Back on the street, she laughed. Shaw was too easy to rile. He would never get to the top. Who would he would talk to now? That sort always tried to cover themselves. As for her own enquiries, she had close to nothing, and she wasn't about to kick off an inter-agency war on the strength of her current case. At least for now.

Chapter 10

The train moved slowly to its terminus at Euston Station and Jack Edwards stood ready to fling open the door and disembark. Why did he always jump when Amanda called? She hadn't said much, but he was bored and her project sounded interesting.

Rail travel wasn't what it used to be. It was faster, cleaner, more comfortable; the food was palatable and the toilets usable. Set against this, though, you couldn't smoke. He got off before the train had stopped, just kept his balance and strode rapidly out of the building. In the poisonous cocktail of London air, he lit a cigarette and sighed with pleasure.

He would have preferred to walk, but with two large bags it wasn't an option and he waited in the taxi line. Normally when in London, Jack used his flat in Sussex Gardens, but as his visits had become less frequent, he had let it out to a couple of American academics.

The Grange Hotel was his favoured alternative. It was small, clean and in a part of town he enjoyed. But this time, Jack gave the taxi driver a name of a large chain hotel in the West End, and after a five-minute drive he was dropped off. He looked at his watch. It was after eight. Just on time, as per Amanda's directions.

He waited in line and at the reception gave his name to a smartly dressed young woman, who flashed him a welcoming smile and introduced herself as Olivia. She confirmed his date of departure a week hence and handed him a key. "Please wait a moment, Mr McLeod. I will arrange for a porter."

He withdrew from the main desk. It had been surprisingly easy to be called McLeod. He watched Olivia. She was in conversation with a colleague now, and a few seconds later she stood alongside him. She grabbed one of his bags and said, "This way, Mr McLeod."

He followed as she led him up some stairs and down a bland corridor to his room. He'd been in worse hotel rooms but not for a long time. On the up side, it had a bed and a bathroom and it was clean.

"Miss Barratt's compliments," Olivia said.

"Yes, I'll thank her later." Jack pointed to the door beside his. "Who's in that room?"

"No one, it'll be empty all week." She handed him the room key, and he deposited the first of his two bags inside.

"This way, Mr McLeod." She glanced at him. "Or should I say Mr Edwards?"

Jack nodded, trying to keep up.

They returned down the stairs. In a small alcove there was a fire door with a typical push-bar opening.

She pushed it open and handed him another key. "This is never alarmed and with this key it can be opened from outside. We are at the rear of the hotel and" – she pointed past a few dustbins – "you can come and go as you please. Okay?"

Jack nodded and Olivia handed him a card with a phone number. "That's me, you can get me any time." She left him to it.

He went back up the stairs and had another look at the room. It hadn't improved, so he locked it and left by the back door.

The route back to civilisation was short, a walk of less than a mile.

The Grange Hotel was quiet and comfortable, and as Jack entered its narrow plush foyer, he was greeted by a young female receptionist of unknown nationality. That she wasn't a local was immediately obvious from her broad, welcoming smile. She backed up her smile with efficiency, and in a very few minutes he had checked in, left his bag in an annex beside the reception and repaired to a comfortable armchair in the small bar area.

He ordered a drink and pulled out a catalogue which showcased lots from an upcoming twentieth-century auction of paintings. He reflected pleasurably on his recent increase in purchasing power. He skipped over pages of paintings that, only a few years earlier, he had coveted. Now even the most expensive works were within his financial reach. He was going to enjoy the auction.

He put down the catalogue, had a mouthful of gin and looked forward to meeting with Amanda, who he was sure would be able to explain why he was now checked into two hotels and sometimes answering to the name of McLeod.

Chapter 11

Cora Samms sat upright on an armchair, her hands clasped in her lap. There was a knock on the door.

"Come."

A silver coffee service was placed alongside her on a rosewood table, and she poured coffee from an elegant Jensen pot. The black coffee steamed a warning that it was not ready to fulfil its destiny, so Cora lit a thin cheroot and stood.

Through the glass of a huge bay window, she stared at the unbroken expanse of the North Atlantic Ocean. Far out, a few erratic seabirds journeyed, who knew where, unaware of and unconcerned with their part in the colossal elemental canvas.

A small spot in the cloudless sky metamorphosed into the recognisable form of her Lear jet. She fixed her gaze on it as, with supreme facility, its elegant form landed and came to a halt at the end of a mile-long concrete strip.

She resumed her seat and sipped some coffee. Another knock on the door signalled the arrival of a tall, middle-aged man.

James Fay was about forty years old, swarthy of complexion and the possessor of the darkest, most impenetrable eyes Cora had ever seen on a human being. His square jaw, powerful physique and short cropped jet-black hair gave him a vaguely Slavic look and an attitude that was, at best, brooding and, at worst, dangerous. Cora had come to understand that his nature was as deep and taciturn as his appearance suggested. He made no move to speak and continued to stand before her, his posture somewhere between attention and ease.

She replaced her delicate coffee cup on the table. She had known him since he was a child. Fay's father had been manager of her father's affairs, and now James fulfilled this role for her.

"Did everything go well?" she asked.

His expression did not vary, nor did his formality relax. "The police have made no further progress. They are convinced it's just another mugging."

"What do we think, James? There is so little time." She indicated a chair opposite and Fay sat. She poured him a coffee and handed it to him.

He took a single mouthful of coffee before beginning. Only the ticking from a grandfather clock interrupted Fay's narration, and after a presentation of some ten minutes, he outlined his recommendation and fell silent.

Cora drew on another cheroot and considered his recommendation for only a few seconds before indicating agreement, and the end of the interview, with a nod.

Chapter 12

On the smaller of the two islets that comprised the Isles of Grace, Captain Nathan Harris lit a cigarette and inhaled deeply. In a perfect world, there wouldn't be a need for a Ministry of Defence. And if there was no MoD, then he wouldn't be sitting on a rickety chair leaning on a flimsy, stained Formica table in an ancient Nissen hut on a barren, rocky islet outcrop in the middle of the North Atlantic Ocean.

He took a slug of cold, black coffee. Time to focus on only positive thoughts. They weren't easy to summon, but he finally settled on the lightness of his duties. But all too soon this had to be reclassified as a negative; on this godforsaken rock, more work might actually be sweet distraction.

Actually, Harris had plenty to do as the continual loathing and distrust of his two management colleagues occupied most of his waking thoughts.

The island posting was headed by John Braid, a half colonel who had almost entirely given up free thought and was obsessed with military bureaucracy. Braid had probably been a good man once, but now there was no one that Harris would less like to rely upon in a tight spot.

Except, that was, for Captain Johnston, the only other army officer on the island. Braid was soft, vague and irrelevant, but at least you could trust him to be all these things. Johnston was hard, certain and decidedly relevant. He was in the army because he believed in the army and its active role in human affairs. If Johnston had his way, the occupant of Downing Street would wear khaki and the state would be engaged in a permanent state of war against the enemy within and without.

Harris wasn't left wing politically. He accepted that the army had a place in society but was not society. Johnston even had a point sometimes about the flabbiness of the state and its people, but his simple, crude and usually violent solutions were distasteful.

Political differences weren't always enough to cause men to dislike each other, and Harris didn't know why he disliked Johnston so much. Certainly, Johnston disliked him, but Johnston disliked virtually everyone so Harris did not feel especially victimised. It was probably Johnston's bloody certainty that he was always right that tipped Harris so decisively against him. Johnston's views were shallow and baseless. Even worse, they were unshakeable. Harris wished he was as certain about one thing as Johnston was about everything.

These reflections were cut short by the unwelcome appearance of both Johnston and Braid. They were an unlikely couple. Johnston was about six and a half feet tall with a lean physique, while Braid, some ten years older at about fifty, was short, stout and looked as if he would be unable to run a hundred yards, let alone fight for Queen and country.

Both men ignored Harris and made their way to a slightly more robust table leaning against the far wall. Upon it sat a huge battered iron kettle containing black, stewed tea. They helped themselves and, after a review of possible seating, they joined Harris.

No mutual acknowledgements followed for, apart from their mutual antipathies, men who spent twenty-four hours a day for close on a year on a two-square-mile island, even army officers, had no need of formalities.

Johnston lit a cigarette, didn't offer one to Harris and then upset the tyrannically anti-smoking Braid by exhaling in his general direction.

Johnston was first to speak, over the top of a two-day-old red-top newspaper. "Fuck, Spurs lost again." He threw down the newspaper, and Braid opened his briefcase and produced three copies of his latest draft monthly report. He tossed a copy to each of them.

"Overall, we are just about on target, gentlemen," he said. "Progress satisfactory and within budget. One or two deliveries have been delayed, but I understand that we can work round this." He gestured at his management team.

Harris said, "Yes, these deliveries have been rescheduled. No real problems."

"Have you both reviewed the management summary?" Braid asked. There were nods. "Well, do either have you have anything to add to this report before I send it off?"

Neither had.

Johnston again reached for the newspaper and Harris started to get up, but Braid checked them both.

"There is one other thing that we need to discuss. Can we please have a look at Section 6?"

Harris sat back down, curious. Section 6 was never discussed, because Section 6 contained no opinions, just facts relating to the stock levels of the key materials on the island. "What about it?"

"Well, I'm not certain, but the plutonium levels look wrong," Braid said. "As far as I can see, none of our activities this month required the use of it. Yet" – he turned a page – "the level is lower this period than last."

Harris and Johnston both returned to the report.

"Quite right, Colonel," Johnston said. "These activities don't require its use."

Harris agreed. "We've probably missed out an activity, or maybe it's a typing error." Stocktaking was undertaken weekly and either he or Johnston were required to sign it off.

"Who signed off the numbers this week?" Braid asked.

Harris put his hand up. "Me. I'll get it re-done."

Unusually for the garrulous Braid, he said nothing, just shut his papers and replaced them in his briefcase. Neither Johnston nor Harris had anything to say and so Braid wound up the meeting.

The discrepancy niggled at Harris. Something wasn't right.

Chapter 13

Tall, slim, with perfect short black hair and piercing blue eyes, Amanda Barratt looked as fabulous as ever. She flashed him a smile as if she knew it. "Hello, Jack." She leant over and kissed him on the cheek and sat down beside him.

"Or should I say 'Mr McLeod'?" She laughed. "Actually, it quite suits you."

"I'll never keep it up," Jack said. "Are you going to tell me why this is necessary?"

"All in good time."

It was tough to hurry Amanda so he didn't bother. "You want a drink?"

"Yes. Coffee. How's your hotel?" she asked.

Jack refused to rise to this. "Nice to see you too."

He looked at her closely. She was about the same age as him, pushing forty, but she had natural beauty and a bone structure which, in a woman of class, allows beauty to endure.

Amanda noisily exhaled a lungful of smoke and said, "Sorry, about the short notice, and sorry about the Mr McLeod thing. Something came up and I thought you would be interested. It's just a minor precaution, probably unnecessary."

He sighed, unconvinced. "Just how dangerous is this project?"

"Hopefully not too much. I just like to be careful."

Not careful enough for his liking. "Well, I'm here as summoned.

What's it all about?"

"What about taking me out tonight?"

Jack was pleasantly surprised by this suggestion. "You brought me to London to take you out?"

"Not exactly," she admitted, "but if I did, would you have come?"

He laughed. "Maybe. What do you fancy doing?"

"Oh, I don't know, anything."

Jack warmed to his task. "I'm not sure what's on, but I'll check – after you tell me why I'm really here."

She took his cue and became business-like. "I've made two appointments for you. You're expected at half past three at the auction house with a man called Singer. Before that, at Brighton Road. It's a government depository full of junk accumulated over many years. They've got the picture and they'll talk you through it all. They'll also give you history and documentation. You are to meet a Mr Rankin. He's not all that happy with my scheme."

"Are you going to show me the picture?" Jack asked.

She reached down to her case and, from inside produced a bulging envelope which she tore open. It contained large colour photographs and a number of typewritten sheets. She retained the sheets and placed the photographs on the table in front of him. They were of high resolution and a first look was all it took to take Jack's breath away.

It could be fake, but he knew it wouldn't be. Dora Maar had been Picasso's soulmate, lover and muse for twenty years and was immortalised in many of the master's works. One such cubist work of Maar had sold for a world-record price at auction, over $100million.

The couple had spent some time in Nazi Germany, although works from this period were rare. Maar was in this picture but in a supporting role, confined to the lower third of the explicit oil and sharing the space with a mass of grotesque symbols, all of which lay squashed and trodden under a long black boot, which belonged to the dominating central figure of the portrait – extreme in angular form and grossly distorted from a human form but, nevertheless, unquestionably Adolf Hitler.

Jack looked skyward and reached for another cigarette, upon which he drew heavily. He scanned the rest of the photographs while Amanda flicked through the pages of her supporting notes.

Jack put the photos down slowly and leant back. "Fucking hell! Is this for real?"

Amanda turned back to the first page of her notes and deliberately re-read a passage before the matter-of-fact "Yes".

Jack picked up and reviewed the photographs again. He did this twice before uttering a loud but tuneless whistle. "Do you know what a sensation this will cause? How the fuck am I going to explain or prove possession of this?"

Amanda laid down the brief, which she had now evidently mastered. "Here's the story. Apparently, a relation of yours – let's say a grandfather – was a businessman working alongside the army in post-war Germany. In payment for certain services, this oil was acquired. The painting had been secured in a private gallery in Germany and, when the Reich fell, it was each man for himself and one of the German officials made off with this painting. So far, so good?"

Jack had a lot of questions, but only managed a slight nod. "Go on."

"Now, this relation of yours, being either very patriotic or very sure that a compulsory confiscation would certainly be made, boxed smartly and cut a deal with the British authorities. In exchange for handing over the picture to the British – apparently no one was interested in publicising its existence – it was agreed that after seventy years, ownership with full rights would revert to his relation or his heirs."

She paused before again dipping into the briefcase and tossing across a letter which, on inspection, proved to be a formal government missive to the effect she had stated.

Jack knew how the story ended. "So now, with seventy-odd years having elapsed, I'm keen to cash in."

"Exactly."

He picked up the photographs again. "Is this picture genuine?"

"Of course," Amanda said.

"You do know that Hitler hated modern art?"

"No, I didn't. Anyway, that's why you're here. You know about these things."

Jack added some further reflections. "If Hitler had seen this work, he would have put his jack boot right through the canvas."

"Well, it's certainly rubbish," Amanda said dismissively. "Looks like a kid did it."

Jack shook his head. Folks either knew about art or they didn't. "The top collectors will not agree with you."

"Yes, so Mr Rankin advised."

"Well, Rankin was right," Jack said. "What's the plan?"

Amanda shrugged. "Put it up for sale, see what happens and then, at the last minute, pull out of the sale."

"Pull out of the sale?" Jack exclaimed.

"Yes, a simple change of mind. After all, you are a collector."

"Well, yes, but not a collector in that league." A complication then occurred to him. "How can I keep it? I can hardly say that I'm going to keep it at home. I'll have art thieves lining up."

Amanda nodded and returned to the briefing notes. "Apparently, you should say that you are giving it back to the government for safe-keeping while considering exhibiting or selling at some future date."

It wasn't a bad answer, but overall, the scheme was fantastic. "Christ, I'm not saying it's impossible, but the publicity will be enormous!"

"Yes, but hopefully for the painting only. You'll be a mystery seller – apparently the auction houses can do a reasonable job on this – at least in terms of keeping you out of the general spotlight. And you are Mr McLeod, after all."

Time to get to the heart of the scheme. "Can you tell me who you're fishing for and what happens if they bite? Look, Amanda, I'm hardly happy about this. I know I owe you and I'll do it, but if this is going to be hairy, I think I have a right to know."

"Yes, I promise you that, but I'll brief you fully later. There's no danger at this stage. Have you ever heard of Cora Samms?" she asked.

"No."

"Hmm, not surprising. She's pretty reclusive, She's a single woman about sixty years old. She's a multi-billionairess, yes billionairess, and she lives on a small group of islands off the Scottish coast. She's connected and she's rumoured to have the finest private art collection in the world."

Jack laughed. "Do people like that really exist – outside of James Bond films?"

"Cora Samms certainly does."

He probed further. "Why do you want to draw her out?"

"An intelligent question at last." Amanda paused and said, "I'm investigating a murder and Samms' company showed up in the investigation. I'd like to find out a bit more about her. Get a bit closer. But it's tricky to do so in the usual way. Samms is reclusive and connected. It's not likely she'd welcome any intrusion."

She paused at this point and Jack, hardly satisfied, asked, "What sort of murder? I mean, who was it?"

"A car salesman, full of drugs and down on his luck. He was knifed to death at the back of King's Cross Station."

"Not your usual caper, surely?"

She nodded but did not say anything further.

Jack was used to Amanda operating on a strict need-to-know basis. It was always frustrating, but she hadn't betrayed his trust yet.

He said, "So the painting smokes out Samms, and then what?"

"Play hard to get. Play very hard to get. In fact, the longer you can string this out and the closer you can get to Samms – and the more you can find out – the better."

Jack shrugged. "Strikes me that there is very little chance that she'll bite."

"Maybe, we will see." She stubbed out her cigarette and finished her drink.

It was time to make a start.

Chapter 14

Jack finished his coffee and ordered a taxi, which arrived promptly. He kissed Amanda on her cheek, promised to call her later, and was soon moving slowly through the central London traffic, heading for Brighton Road.

The building proved easy enough to locate. The front of the unprepossessing brick façade was adorned with a slightly corroded plate which stated that the building was home to a branch of the Government Surplus Unit.

Before a glass-panelled door, a prominent button invited visitors to press. Jack did so and was admitted to a small, plainly furnished foyer where he asked for Mr Rankin. The teenage attendant invited him to sit down, and a few moments later a youngish, tall, clean-shaven man in casual dress shook Jack by the hand and invited him through a small side door, which led to a lift. Rankin selected the lowest button on the lift control. "The basement," he said to Jack.

From the outside, the building presented three storeys, but, like so many government buildings, the bulk of the accommodation was subterranean.

The lift doors opened into a surprisingly bright and dust-free open space. It contained well-spaced shelving around the walls and a variety of boxes and crates, which gave an appearance of method and order.

They sat either side of a modern desk. Rankin undertook a silent review of a selection of paperwork. After a few minutes, he threw them aside and fixed his gaze on Jack. "Right, Mr McLeod, basically we will spend the next hour or so assessing, or perhaps appreciating, the painting. After this, I understand that you will travel to the auctioneers to discuss the sale arrangements."

"Fine," Jack said impatiently. "Where's the painting?"

"Over there. I'll get it shortly, but we are waiting for our expert to arrive. Professor Dunmore will be here presently."

Jack and Rankin sat silently for about a minute before the distant, then gathering sound of the lift signalled that the professor had arrived. Jack turned at the approaching footsteps and knew that the man coming towards them was Dunmore. Only academics wore pullovers under a suit.

Rankin introduced them. Dunmore was a celebrated academic, a holder of a chair relating to modern art, and a knight of the realm. Jack was Jack McLeod.

Rankin said with an air of reluctance, "I'll get the painting." He rose and returned with the oil, which he carefully placed upon the desk, and leant against the facing wall.

Although Jack had seen the photographs, the sight of the real thing sent a frisson of excitement through his body. The frame was old, dusty and plain, but the frame didn't matter. The oil was mesmeric. The vivid colours and near impossible angles, especially of the central image, assaulted his senses. He couldn't pull his gaze from it.

He was still staring at the painting as Dunmore launched into a dry lecture which, when stripped of academic pretensions, created a narrative around the features and symbols. Dunmore appeared in little doubt that they were all designed by the genius of an artist to satirise an idiot of a dictator.

Jack, however, wasn't so sure, and at the end of the lecture was undecided whether the work was in homage or revulsion. There was little else he could profitably learn from further academic review. "Okay, I think I've got all that," he said to Rankin.

Rankin nodded and thanked Dunmore for his time, whereupon the academic left without further comment.

Rankin returned to the pile of papers on the desk. He sniffed.

"I am instructed to give you the following documents."

Archivists didn't like handing out archive materials. "I can't think why duplicates aren't sufficient," he added. "Anyway …"

He counted out four documents: three signed statements from army officers and a bill of sale to a Mr Archibald McLeod.

Rankin said, "The first three of these are genuine. Of course, Mr Archibald McLeod is, we understand, the name of your paternal grandfather. The bill of sale is obviously fake."

Jack leafed through the first three documents. "These are the guys who found this?"

"Yes, Mr McLeod. Please make sure you return the documents."

Chapter 15

With Jack gone, Amanda had another cup of coffee in the small rear gardens of the Grange Hotel. A moment later she was joined by another man. "Sit down, Peter."

The young long-legged man sat awkwardly on the metal garden seat.

"Coffee?"

"No thanks, ma'am."

"What have you got?"

Peter had two folders. From the first he read, "Jimmy Trent. Aged forty-two. Ex-army, Guards and special forces. He made captain and he was non-commissioned. Record really good. He finished after twenty years and started Prestige Cars. No criminal record. Nothing else at this stage, ma'am."

"And Hunt?"

"Doctor Jasper Hunt, fifty-seven. He's been a general practitioner for about twenty years. He started quite late in life. Before that it's a bit hazy, but he worked for some drug companies. The word is that he's a gambler and a bit of a womaniser. Two times divorced. He was up before the British Medical Association once. There was a suggestion he was too close to a drug company. Oversubscribing, that sort of thing. But he was cleared."

"Did you tail him?" Amanda asked.

"Yes, ma'am."

"And?"

"He left about half an hour after your visit. He drove out west to Walton. He's a fast driver. I could have stopped him at any time."

She laughed. "Where did he go?"

"To a house near the river. A cottage, nice place. It was tough to keep up and keep hidden."

"But you managed it?" She really hoped so.

"Yes, ma'am. He met a woman."

"A patient?"

"I don't think so, otherwise he'll be back up before the BMA. They were kissing and cuddling on the doorstep. Couldn't keep their hands off each other. He was there overnight. He left at about five this morning and returned to his home in London."

"And who was the girl?" Amanda asked.

Peter reconsulted his notes. "The house is owned by a Doctor Laura Gibson, ma'am."

"A fellow general practitioner?"

"No, ma'am, she's a government scientist in the Ministry of Defence."

Whatever else Amanda had expected to learn from her speculative decision to tail Hunt, it wasn't this.

"Do you need information on Dr Gibson, ma'am?" Peter asked.

"Yes, everything you can get."

"Pick her up?"

"No, not at the moment," she said. "Tell Bradley. Say I wasn't happy with Hunt and he and his girlfriend are behaving suspiciously. Encourage him to talk to them. See what he comes up with."

She reached into her bag. "This cheque and this bank account. Get on to this. I want to know who this salesman is and how he has access to Samms Corporation money. Give it to Max and tell him it's urgent."

"And Mr Edwards?"

"Keep close, very close, Peter. I don't want him out of your sight."

Chapter 16

A fifteen-minute taxi journey took Jack to the head office of the world's premier auctioning house. He spent most of that time reminding himself that today his name was McLeod. Viewing was by appointment only. He had an appointment so he pushed the button.

"I'm here to see Mr Singer," Jack announced when the door opened.

"Certainly, sir, this way."

The immediate area widened into a low-ceilinged gallery, which was home to a number of artworks with which Jack was familiar. "Are these the lots for the upcoming twentieth-century sale?"

"Yes, sir."

"I'd like to have a quick look."

"Certainly, sir." The assistant withdrew a few paces to sit on a chair.

Jack knew what he was looking for and he soon located the JD Fergusson oil. It was big, bright and vibrant, a scene of Parisian café society before the first war. He liked it, he liked it a lot. He would bid. The estimate of £200,000 was fair value, but he might go higher.

He returned to the assistant, who now directed him through a narrow corridor and to an office door which bore a plate stating 'A. Singer, Director'. The assistant knocked and entered. "Mr McLeod, sir."

Singer was a slightly built man of about thirty-five dressed in a near black suit. He appeared of foreign extraction and his short, black, greased-down hair gave him the appearance of a 1930s dancing host plying his trade at a moderately fashionable seaside hotel.

He introduced himself as Andre, and, with enthusiasm, beckoned Jack into his large and comfortable office and invited him to sit on a leather horseshoe sofa surrounding a glass table.

Singer poured coffee for them both and then sat alongside him.

You weren't allowed to smoke in any workplace or public place these days, but you could when you had a painting worth $100million for sale. Andre produced an ashtray, and, as Jack inhaled, he produced the buff folder which contained the documents that Rankin had reluctantly given up. The auction director placed the papers carefully on the table and reviewed them.

"You haven't brought the picture?" he said with disappointment.

"Oh, it's being retrieved from storage as we speak. A day or two at most."

"Good. I am looking forward to seeing it. As for the potential sale, everything's looking good at the moment, Mr McLeod. Although the market is difficult, interest has been immense, as one might expect for such a unique piece. Estimating, however, is difficult and prospective purchasers do tend to keep their intentions to themselves. We are dealing here with very rich people who know the art business, but I should say that we expect to be close to the upper estimate."

Singer paused and looked intently at Jack who, at this moment and despite the good news, had very little to say. What sort of people could afford to pay north of $100million for a painting? There were all sorts of associated moral questions, but they were all too big, and he returned to Singer, who was looking at him expectantly.

"Mr McLeod? I hope this is satisfactory?"

Jack realised he was seeking positive feedback on his company's marketing efforts. If you couldn't market and publicise an original Picasso oil of Adolf Hitler then you might as well give up, but it wasn't the time to say so. "Yes, very good, Mr Singer."

Singer seemed satisfied with this endorsement and moved smoothly on to the contract details. He passed Jack a small document which contained even smaller writing and began a rapid summary of the key contractual details. Pushing forward an expensive-looking pen, he said, "There only remains the question of commission, Mr McLeod. I have left that section blank."

Jack was in uncharted territory. Auction commissions were usually up to twenty percent, but if you were a big buyer you could get five percent. This was different.

"Mmmm."

Singer was ever helpful and proffered his pen again. "You sign here, Mr McLeod."

"Yes, thanks, Mr Singer, I have a pen."

Singer beamed broadly and holstered his pen.

"The thing is, Mr Singer," Jack said, "I've been having a few further thoughts on this sale."

Singer was still smiling.

"'I'm comfortably off. I don't really need the money, and over the last few days I've been thinking about how unique this picture really is. I mean, luck and fate have given me title to something amazing. How else would I own something like this?'

Singer's smile was fading now but he made no attempt to interject. Jack concluded, "So I think that I'd like to hold on to it for a while."

"Yes, I see what you mean, Mr McLeod, and, if you are resolved, then of course you must do as you say." There was something in his tone, just the right side of patronising, that suggested a "but" was coming Jack's way.

"It is not only hard to purchase and acquire such priceless

treasures but also, Mr McLeod, difficult to own them. I mean that, while the existence of this work was unknown, things were different."

Jack slowly nodded, starting to grasp Singer's argument.

"You see, owning a piece such as this now, unless you should house it in some permanent and public establishment, is a very demanding task. Lighting, heating and ambience are critical; and then, of course, there is" – he coughed politely – "security."

"Yes, I can see that—" Jack began.

"With respect, Mr McLeod, I wonder if you do? Obviously, you have what is, by most measures, a high-quality collection of works, but this work is, I hope you will forgive me saying, in an entirely different league. In summary, I would say your options are either selling or permanent display in public galleries."

Singer paused and then added, "Also, Mr McLeod, having perused the indicative offers, I would say, although I cannot be sure, there is a good possibility that at this time you could realise significantly over our estimate. There are some wealthy and determined individuals who are very interested in your picture. I wouldn't be surprised if the price goes to $150million."

Jack screwed up his face. What path would he choose if he owned the work? He couldn't decide and re-focused on his assignment. "Well, Mr Singer, I'm sure you are right, but at this moment I just don't think I want to part with it."

For the first time, Singer's face exhibited some disappointment. Jack moved to reassure him. "Of course, any expenses you have incurred, plus some extra, I'll be happy to pay."

"Yes, thank you, but I should tell you that it is not quite so easy to completely close this matter."

"Why not?"

"Well, some of these collectors will undoubtedly try to contact you with a view to a private purchase."

Jack said, "That might be okay."

"If you wish, I could arrange meetings with the most interested parties?"

"Who are they?"

Singer hesitated and Jack said with resolution, "Mr Singer, I'm pretty much determined not to sell, but if I were to reconsider, I will certainly not sell to an unknown party!"

Singer hesitated again and then appeared to relent, for he rose and, after retrieving another folder from his desk, peered into its secrets.

"I would say that there are three serious potential buyers."

Jack nodded appreciatively when, in hushed tones, Singer told him of the interest of a Middle Eastern billionaire and an American industrial tycoon. Jack nodded as if the first two names were familiar to him. The third name meant nothing either.

"Who is James Fay?" he asked.

Singer confessed that he was not sure, but added, "Mr Fay is acting as a representative for another."

"Who?"

"That will be for Mr Fay to confirm. However, I understand that Mr Fay represents Miss Cora Samms."

Jack affected to be ignorant of this name also. Singer went on, "I am not surprised you haven't heard of Cora Samms. While she is not well known to the public she is, I would say, probably the most serious and determined collector of all."

"Oh."

"Actually, Mr Fay will be here this afternoon. Would you like me to arrange a meeting?"

Jack was warming to his assignment and said breezily, "Well, I have given you my current thoughts. However, if Mr Fay has personally travelled to discuss this sale, it would be discourteous not to meet with him."

***

After a moderate lunch in an expensive establishment, Jack returned to the auction house and made his way back to Singer's office.

Again, his knock was answered promptly, and he was shown to his usual seat. Already there was a tall, sturdy man of about forty-five. He had black eyes and he looked dangerous. Singer introduced them, arranged coffee, and left.

Jack calmly considered his companion, picturing him as a potential adversary. It was an uncomfortable thought and he let it pass as Fay proffered a business card which read, "James Fay, Samms Corporation"

When he spoke, James Fay was impressively brief. "Mr Singer tells me you propose to withdraw your Picasso from the auction. I represent the Samms Corporation and am authorised to make you an offer to purchase the picture."

"I have already stated that I do not wish to sell," Jack said.

Fay ignored this. "The picture is estimated at $100 million. The Samms Corporation will offer you a minimum of $115 million and more if an independent estimate states a higher fair value. We would, of course, agree on an independent valuer. For this, we would expect a period of exclusive negotiation rights."

Fay took a sip of coffee.

"That's a handsome offer, Mr Fay, but I can only re-state that I have no wish to sell." Jack was quite enjoying this now. He knew Fay would improve the offer.

Fay sat forward a little and did so Jack. "I am authorised to increase the minimum guaranteed purchase price to $125 million, Mr McLeod."

The use of the word "authorised" marked Fay out as an inferior negotiator and Jack, with appropriate appreciation, again turned down the offer.

Fay had now apparently run out of script and, after a period of silence, he excused himself from the room. Jack finished off his coffee and lit a cigarette. In a few minutes, James Fay returned and resumed his seat. Jack prepared to receive his best and final offer.

This time the offer was not monetary. Fay said, "Miss Cora Samms, the head of the Samms Corporation, is eager to continue these discussions and she wishes me to invite you to be her guest at dinner."

"Well, I have no objections to a short meeting with Miss Samms," Jack said. "Is she in London?"

Fay's impenetrable features momentarily gave way to what was almost a smile. "Unfortunately, Miss Samms is unable to leave her home at present. She invites you to join her there."

"Where is home?"

"Miss Samms lives on a private island off the north-west coast of Scotland."

"What? Look, it's me who's selling. Are you seriously telling me that I am expected to go to an island somewhere out in the Atlantic?"

Fay seemed unfazed. "Miss Samms would be delighted if you would be her guest. The Isles of Grace is a spectacular location, and I am sure you would enjoy the experience."

It was all pretty surreal, and a reasonable man would want more information. Jack thought for a moment and said, "I'd like to speak to Mr Singer."

Fay nodded. He left the room and was replaced by Singer.

"I have discussed this matter with Mr Fay," Jack said. "I am still disinclined to sell. However, Mr Fay has invited me to visit Miss Samms for a further discussion. I must say it all sounds intriguing, but before today I had never heard of Miss Samms. Can you tell me something about her?"

Singer spoke with confidence. "Miss Samms has been known to us as a valued client, perhaps our most valued client, for over thirty years. I should add that her family have been clients of ours since our founding."

He stopped at this point, apparently satisfied that no further endorsement was necessary.

It was time to bite. "Well, it sounds interesting. Now, where are these Isles of Grace?"

Singer rose and readmitted Fay, who was carrying a folded

document which proved to be a map. He deliberately unfolded it and placed it on the table. His finger left the mainland, crossed the ocean and eventually halted at a small island. "The Isles of Grace, Mr McLeod."

"How long to get there?" Jack asked.

Fay said, "Not more than two hours."

"Two hours?" he exclaimed.

"Yes, sir. Miss Samms has a private plane."

"Well, when? I have a number of appointments here in London."

"Whenever you wish, sir. The invitation is an open one. We could go tomorrow?"

Jack heard himself saying, "Why not?"

The meetings were over. Jack had done well, but his head was thumping. Amanda had said there was no danger, but, if that were true, why was he going around London with a fake name and trying to sell a picture he didn't own? The Isles of Grace were a long way from anywhere. He had, at least, remembered to arrange tomorrow's pick-up – not from the Grange, but from the Park Lane hotel, a precaution which now made more sense.

He rang Amanda. Annoyingly, she was busy and had no time to talk. It was disappointing, because there was plenty to tell. She just said, "I'll see you tonight as planned."

Until then Jack was a free man, free to worry about James Fay and the power of the Samms Corporation.

Chapter 17

Amanda rang off. Jack had made progress, but so had Bradley. He had managed to get an autopsy report turned around quickly and he had a pile of papers in front of him which he announced were copies of Ash Ashanti's bank statements.

Bradley snorted and coughed, and then started with the gory details. "He was drunk and full of drugs. He died from a single stab wound to the neck. Something very sharp and very thin."

Amanda said, "Like what? Some kind of knife?"

Bradley shook his head. "Not really sure. Stiletto, maybe even a letter opener. A narrow blade."

He moved on to the bank statements. "These are more interesting. Very volatile. Our man was a big spender. A million-pound overdraft limit, but he seems to have used it. We've got a year's worth of statements, and the ins and – mostly – the outs have grown over the period."

"Drugs?"

"Could be – a lot of cash drawings, increasingly frequent. Seems that his drawings from the garage accounts were also on the up – some big withdrawals recently. I phoned Trent. Apparently only a single signature was required."

"Interesting," she said. It wasn't the sort of thing that a business six months overdue with its VAT could stand. "So, he was bleeding the business. And almost certainly collecting deposits or other payments and not handing them over?"

"Could be."

"Could Trent not keep him out of the accounts? Change signatures?"

Bradley shook his head. "Seems it wasn't that easy. They were fifty/fifty partners: any change would have needed both of them to agree."

"Could you see Trent killing him for that?"

"Not really, although at this rate the business would have been a goner soon enough."

"Maybe he was going to pay money back with that cheque."

Bradley looked doubtful. "Maybe."

Amanda shuffled through the sheets of transactions. Payments to gyms and a lot to designer clothing stores. No sign of the Samms Corporation, and the rest of the deposits were unremarkable.

And then she halted at an entry. She had seen that before. She turned back the sheets. There were about six credits in all, made on the same day of each of the last six months. They weren't the biggest payments, but why would the West End Medical practice be paying one of their patients £10,000 per month?

Chapter 18

Jack sat in Amanda's flat. An art deco clock struck seven and he got up and returned to the bottles of spirits. He was trying to become a non-drinker these days, having taken the pledge some three or four years ago. Today he had done a decent day's work. He poured himself a long gin and tonic. He took a mouthful and noted with disapproval the selection of prints which covered the walls.

She came in. She was always smart, always perfectly dressed, but this time she had surpassed herself and she looked more attractive than he had ever seen her.

She spoke in soft, cultured tones. "Don't I get a drink?"

He moved back to the spirits, mixed and handed her a drink. He pointed at the prints.

"Do you like them?" she asked.

He laughed. "No, they're terrible."

She shrugged. "Oh well, I quite like them. They go well here."

"We need to go in fifteen minutes. You want to hear about today, or will we wait?"

She considered. "We'll wait, I think. Let's just do something normal tonight. At least for a couple of hours." She leant forward. "Now what have you got planned for me?"

"Oh, just a play and a bit of supper. Nothing too exciting."

She smiled. "Oh good, I've got quite enough excitement in my life."

The doorbell pealed and they got up. She stood and looked at him. Then she extended her arm. He took it and squeezed it a little in return, then walked out into the London night with the sexiest woman in town.

***

The play was good and so was the supper. At about eleven, Jack and Amanda returned to her flat. She opened the door. He hesitated.

"Come on," she said. "I need to hear about your day."

She poured both of them a drink and sat alongside him. It was business now so it would have been easier if she sat further away, but he let her stay.

"I have an appointment tomorrow," he said.

"With who?"

"Cora Samms."

She whistled. He thought a compliment was in order, and she managed one. Then her face hardened. "Where are you meeting her?"

Jack sipped some gin. "At her lair. On a fucking island somewhere off Scotland. I'd have been nearer if I was at home."

"Wow. How on earth did you swing that?" She moved to a seat opposite him. All business now.

"It was easy, too easy really. Her man was at the auction house, someone called Fay, James Fay. You were right, it seems this painting is irresistible. He offered me $125 million dollars."

"Cheapskate," she interjected, laughing." Did you take it?"

He laughed back. "I turned him down a few times, and then he invited me to meet her. I leave tomorrow morning. Did you know she lives on an island?"

"Well, I did, but I didn't expect this. Anyway, this is good, much better."

"Better for who?" Jack asked.

"Come on, I promised you an interesting time."

That was true enough. "So, what do you want me to do?" he

asked. "Just go along? Observe and report?"

Amanda said, "Yes, essentially, but there's a few more things that you need to know."

He felt a frisson of anxiety. "Oh, like what? You got more information on this killing?"

"Not really. Ash Ashanti, former socialite and lately drug-using down-and-out. He owed money to everyone. We've interviewed his doctor, who confirmed that he was a drug user. The business partner has an alibi, and we're not yet finished talking to everyone that might have known him. He once had a lot of so-called friends: girlfriends, C-list celebrities, that sort of thing. But at the end he was pretty much friendless. We'll get around them all eventually and keep rattling the tree but, really, I'm not much further on."

"No other evidence?"

"Nothing from the scene," she said. "The strongest probability is simply a murderous flare-up with another street-dweller over God knows what. Maybe a mugging - everything was taken."

"Well, if that's true, it sounds like you'll never solve it."

"Maybe not. But there's another reason I'm interested in Samms."

"The real reason?"

"Well, potentially a more important reason."

Jack put his drink down. "Okay, let's have it."

Amanda said airily, "There's a British Army facility on the island that we lease from Samms."

Jack groaned. "What sort of facility?"

"All top secret, but bomb research mostly."

That covered a lot of possibilities. "That's a long way away for research."

"Yes, it's extremely sensitive. Both the nature of the research and, well, even its existence."

Jack shut his eyes for a moment.

"Honestly, I don't know much more than that myself at the moment. Anyway, that shouldn't really matter from your point of view. It's on the other side of the island. You don't need to go there or do anything. Just go and visit Samms and talk about art. Don't even mention the army facility, and I'll take it from there."

Jack said sourly, "Well, that sounds easy enough."

"Yes. However, if you do run into Colonel Braid, he's the commanding officer of the base. Tell him you are a friend of Andrew Baxter. That is, if you are alone with him."

"Who's Baxter?"

"He works with me. He knows Braid. Don't say anything else. Anyway, I doubt you will run into him."

At this, she got up and kissed him lightly on the cheek. "I've had a lovely evening, but it's late and you've got an early start tomorrow."

And a whole lot of new information to process.

Chapter 19

The Artemis Club was housed in an impressive stand-alone building in Mayfair and it was very much part of the fabric of what many called "the establishment".

Andrew Baxter didn't like places like this, but this appointment was less of a meeting and more of a summons, and the choice of venue had been out of his control. As he walked past Corinthian columns and into a high-domed reception area, he reflected on places like this and their part in modern Western history. Wars started, fortunes made and lost, and the fate of many decided as the members passed the port.

He waited at a prepossessing reception. Although the club's influence might have waned, the complacent splendour of its architecture was undiminished. An ancient male receptionist eventually attended him and, after a long time, led him at a snail's pace up endless broad marble stairs. At the head of the staircase, a set of high and heavy wooden doors awaited.

They were guarded also, and he was handed over to an even older member of staff, who led him inside. The room was richly carpeted and home to numerous irregular table and chair combinations. At a discreet small alcove area, the attendant stopped and indicated a chair.

Sitting opposite was the source of his summons: a tall, lean and strong man of about sixty dressed in a regulation but stylish pinstriped suit. It was just after eleven in the morning, but time didn't really exist in the Artemis Club and the man ordered brandies, which were promptly delivered.

Britain's top spy took a long draught of the spirit and looked pleasantly at Baxter. Theoretically the two men were peers, being head of their respective services, but among the unwritten understandings of the British constitution, the Director was primus inter pares, and this slight advantage in rank gave him close to absolute power.

The Director got straight to the point. "Nice of you to come along, Andrew."

As if Baxter had had a choice.

"Thing is, I wanted a word with you. Nothing serious, really, but I was speaking to Colonel Shaw - you know him?"

Without waiting for confirmation, he continued. "Colonel Shaw runs a few research programmes for us. Good man, Shaw. Anyway, I ran into him yesterday and he mentioned that he'd been chatting with one of your girls. A Miss Barratt."

Baxter wondered what Amanda would say to being classified this way. "Yes, Amanda's on secondment to the Home Office at the moment. Not sure what she's working on."

"It seems she is investigating a killing. A squalid business down King's Cross way. A tramp or down-and-out?" The Director stared at Baxter.

"Oh, I believe I heard about that. Routine affair, surely?"

"Well I would have thought so, but it seems your girl was asking about Cora Samms. Do you know her?"

"I've heard the name, I think. That's all."

"She is very low profile, practically off the radar. Lives on an island somewhere in the Atlantic. She's been useful to us in the past, giving us use of some of her land. Funnily enough, we're talking to her at the moment about extending our leasing arrangements. Actually" – he lowered his voice –" negotiations are at a delicate stage and I want to make sure that nothing upsets her. Shouldn't take more than a month or so. After that, do what you like."

It all seemed very reasonable and the request had been delivered as if the whole thing was of the most marginal concern. But if the Director was involved, then concern would hardly be marginal. "Okay, fine," Baxter said.

The Director nodded back and emptied his brandy. "Fancy another?" and again didn't wait for an answer. "Of course not. I expect you are far too busy to sit and chew the fat with me." He cast a glance in the direction of an alert waiter and ordered a large brandy, this time for only himself.

Baxter rose.

"Thanks, Andrew," the Director added by way of farewell, and then resumed his attention on his newly arrived brandy and the broadsheet newspaper which had sat on his knees throughout the interview.

At least the interview had been a short one, and Baxter was soon out of the pretentious club and striding purposefully through the London streets.

The request was clear and it was simple. All he had to do was to tell "one of his girls" to leave things alone for a month. He laughed silently.

Amanda Barratt was no one's girl. He would let her get on with it, because, despite having risen so high in his profession, he had a secret weakness: he had never been much good at taking orders.

Chapter 20

Jack was tiring of residing at two hotels but he would do what Amanda told him. Mostly because she was quite right.

The Park Lane hotel was only about a ten-minute walk from the Grange and he was now familiar with a regular routine of leaving from and returning to Park Lane, spending a short time there, sometimes ordering some room service, roughing up the bed, and then heading back to the Grange. This discipline seemed necessary this morning. He was meeting Fay at seven thirty.

He had a shower and, a little after five, he left the Grange and walked to the scruffy rear entrance of the Park Lane hotel. He had clothes there so, once there, he could relax. Time for another couple of hours sleep.

This worked well as he woke again at seven refreshed and ready for the day ahead.

Fay would be punctual, he knew. At twenty past seven, he finished a light breakfast and selected a seat in the reception area well away from the main entrance, but allowing an uninterrupted view outside. From behind a newspaper, he watched as a large black Mercedes swept in and halted near the entrance. The driver got out. He didn't look like a driver. He was solidly built, although this was less obvious owing to him being about six and a half feet tall. His hair was closely cropped, and, despite his casual demeanour, his eyes repeatedly scanned the immediate vicinity. He looked armed.

A moment later Fay was in the reception, and he was talking with familiarity to a cloakroom attendant. He nodded and handed the man something, then scanned the reception area.

Jack kept the newspaper in front of his face and watched as Fay moved to the reception and started talking to a receptionist. The receptionist picked up a phone. Jack had seen enough and moved to Fay.

"Good morning, Mr Fay."

"Good morning, Mr McLeod," Fay responded. "Are you ready?"

Jack nodded and followed him outside.

On sighting them, the driver moved rapidly to open the rear door. This done, without a word he returned to the driver's seat and, after effortlessly executing a full U-turn on the gridlocked Bloomsbury road, they were soon speeding north against the traffic.

Throughout this journey, Fay, sitting alongside, although not near, given the capacious nature of the Mercedes, indicated various comforts at Jack's disposal.

It was way too early for a drink so he demurred, although he accepted the proffered newspaper and nodded appreciatively at the emergence of a sliding ashtray from the console in front.

Fay apparently had no need of any comforts and simply said that they would arrive at the private airfield within half an hour. This advised, he relapsed into his seat and stared directly ahead with his dead black eyes.

The whole scenario was indisputably surreal, but despite the latent menacing power of his hosts, Jack decided to relax and try to take things as they came. He checked his racing emotions easily enough in the comfort of his surroundings and managed to relax until, within the promised time, the car turned off the main road and powered down a smooth single-track tree-lined road.

The last part of the route was unmarked, but the quality of the road suggested the facility was expensive. This was confirmed as the car came to a halt at a barrier and was then ushered through by a young, well-dressed man about as far away from an archetypal gateman as Jack could have imagined. The closely planted line of fir trees ended abruptly and was replaced with dense, colourful shrubbery, and this gave way to a sparsely populated car park outside the aerodrome's terminal.

The car stopped, and Fay held the door open. Jack followed Fay and the driver into the modern-looking administrative building and sat in a small reception area with coffee, while Fay and his driver moved to where a suited receptionist sat behind a desk.

On their return, Fay said, "The airplane is ready, Mr McLeod."

Jack followed them through an adjoining door and, after a few hundred yards of nondescript corridor, emerged onto a runway. A moment later, he was sitting comfortably on a Lear jet, occupying a single seat in a circular arrangement of four.

Fay and the driver withdrew through a curtained area and the engines roared into life. Fay returned, strapped Jack in and placed a drink before him.

"The weather's fine, Mr McLeod. Our flight should be one and a half hours." He flicked on a colossal flat-screen television, placed the control in front of Jack and indicated a button which he bade him press if he had need of assistance. He withdrew behind the curtain which cordoned off the front of the plane. The smooth power of the aircraft took it rapidly to a cruising altitude, and Jack was on his way.

Chapter 21

On Lessor, the smaller of the two islets of the Isles of Grace, Captain Nathan Harris strode powerfully over the broken ground and through swishing waist-high wild grasses. It was a good day to be out and about. The sun was strong and the views of the foaming ocean were unbroken in every direction.

When Harris was in the right mood – which wasn't often these days – he thought the island was the most beautiful place in the world. A zephyr of wind, maybe twenty miles per hour, about as low as it ever got, cooled his face.

At the highest point of the islet he stopped and stood close to the exposed ridge. Far out to sea, naturally engineered gannets hunted with elegance and efficiency. Harris was a scientist, and a good one, but he couldn't build anything as good as them.

He lit a morning cigarette. He looked across to Main, and Cora Samms' brilliant white art deco mansion. Although he didn't want to like it, he did.

Harris was thinking about the morality of his science. One man's security was potentially another's destruction, and, if his bombs were ever used in anger, morally he was in it up to his neck. He gave himself a break with an easy lie. If not him, others would undertake the work.

He decided to continue the walk, and contemplated taking a route to the ravine between the islets, but changed his mind when he spied the form of his colleague Captain Johnston approaching the causeway from the opposite islet.

Moments spent with Johnston were far too many and mostly uncongenial, and Harris had no wish to spoil his free time with a voluntary meeting, so he lit another cigarette and sat on the broken rocky ground on the clifftop and watched his colleague.

Johnston's massive figure made steady progress to the bridge over the causeway and he negotiated it sure-footedly. He barely broke stride when ascending the steep slopes back to the base and Harris felt a sneaking admiration for his conditioning. As an opponent, Johnston would be formidable.

Bad as their relationship was, at least they were on the same side, and that had to be a good thing. If only he could find it in himself to agree with Johnston and not find him too irritating. For a moment, gazing out to sea, Harris thought he might give it a go, but a glance at his wristwatch saw this resolution blown as he cursed; he was five minutes late for an unwanted meeting with Johnston and Braid.

He threw his cigarette into the North Atlantic and headed, more slowly now, back towards the facility just in time to grudgingly hold open the door for the far-from-breathless Johnston. In silence, the captains made their way to Braid's office.

A sharp knock was answered with a swift "Come" and they entered and took seats alongside Braid at his battered meeting table.

Braid handed out a single sheet of paper to each of the captains and allowed them a few seconds to digest its contents. "Gentlemen, these figures speak for themselves. There can be no doubt that we have a serious problem."

Neither Harris nor Johnston said anything.

"As I see it, we need to deal with this formally. But I don't want headquarters all over this just yet. Therefore, we need one final, urgent investigation. If we can't clear this discrepancy in a day or two, then I'm afraid it's an audit – from outside."

Harris then spoke and probably – for once – spoke for Johnston also. "Who's to lead this enquiry?"

"I'd like both of you to cooperate on this. Report back to me in two days." He looked hard at them both, rose and said, "Any questions?"

Harris and Johnston had none, and the meeting was over.

Chapter 22

Braid watched as the two men left his office and wondered what turn events would now take. That his two captains disliked each other was clear, but how far would this antipathy go? Surely, they would be able to work together? If the plutonium was missing, then it had to be found. Even if it was found, he was pretty much finished, especially if the loss had to be reported to the MoD. A career in the army was over if you left your briefcase on a train with no more than the stationery order, and a dim view would be taken of the loss of enough plutonium to make several nuclear bombs – and their smart devices.

Rogue and even non-rogue states would bid high for this material. He might be remembered as a man who single-handedly presided over the demolition of decades of nuclear non-proliferation treaties. It was, at least, a surprising outcome for a career that had been heading for a bland and undistinguished ending.

Braid dredged up an image from some thirty summers ago when he had passed out at Sandhurst. Where had that man gone? Hopes, aspirations and a desire to do something useful with his life. He had, it was true, no specific objectives, but as he looked at himself, puffy, overweight and stuck on a remote island, he was pretty sure that none of this had been part of the plan.

With a wave of resolution, he determined that neither had he planned to fuck up the defence of the realm. Driven thus, he reviewed the situation. The plutonium was either missing or it wasn't; the figures were either right or they were wrong. If the plutonium was missing, where was it? Furthermore, who had it or had stolen it was just as big a question.

Outsiders could be ruled out, so that just left insiders, and that was the most uncomfortable truth of all. The handling and recording of the material were covered by what had seemed like unbreakable safeguards requiring multiple signatures at every stage. Carelessness maybe, but, more likely, collaboration and conspiracy.

His radio was broken and the two back-up satellite phones were missing. Braid was on his own and his command was severely compromised.

Chapter 23

After declining a third large brandy, Jack got up from the club chair, looked out of the jet's windows and scanned uninterrupted miles of the North Atlantic Ocean. He wondered why he had never heard of the Isles of Grace and why, in a world permeated by a 24/7 intrusive media, its very existence was still under the radar.

A moment later, James Fay emerged and advised that the weather was fine and they would be landing on the island in about five minutes. Jack managed to strap himself in this time, and, with an easy confidence he didn't feel, braced for the descent, which was smooth and uneventful, save for the visual shock of the sudden emergence of land. The view from the window changed, and they sped by what looked like rows of crops until the jet eventually halted.

"Did you have a pleasant flight, Mr McLeod?" James Fay asked when he appeared again.

Jack got up and stretched. "Yes, very good."

Outside the jet, the immediate view was a disappointment. The narrow airstrip was cut into the land, making the crops on either side artificially high. To his left, about a thousand yards distant, a bland, brilliant white gable end of what he imagined to be the principal residence also blocked the view. Fay walked into a large open shed and emerged with an electric buggy usually found on golf courses. Jack jumped in.

Fay halted before a low, metallic fence and indicated that Jack should alight. "Miss Samms is in the garden, sir." With that, he sped off round the back of the house.

Jack took a few hesitant steps towards the fence and proceeded through a gap. The concrete below his feet changed to short-cut grass and a moment later he was assailed by a view as stunning as anything he had ever seen.

On his right, the façade of the house was gradually revealed as a flat-roofed two-storey monument to the art deco movement. It was an impressive and massive construction, made more remarkable by its situation and, no doubt, the engineering and construction efforts so obviously needed, but for Jack it was the remaining 270 degrees of the panorama which compelled him.

It was before noon, and the sun was still short of its full summer height, but it was powerful enough to illuminate an impressive range of blue-green tones of the unbroken ocean. He knew in an instant why someone would live here, especially a reclusive billionairess.

He took a few slow steps forward. Ahead, the vista was interrupted by a tiny silhouetted figure standing at the far edge of the lawns.

He knew it would be Samms.

She turned her head as he approached, and Jack regarded a fine-looking, exceedingly slim woman of some sixty years.

She looked at him, proffered her hand and spoke in near perfect aristocratic English. "Good morning, Mr McLeod, I am Cora Samms. Welcome to my home."

Although Jack had indeed performed a service in answering her summons, he heard himself say, "Thank you for inviting me. You have a wonderful home."

She inclined her head and then began to walk across the lawn.

Where the grass ended, a flat concreted area began, which proved to be the beginning of a wide but precipitous road down to an impressively large and modern harbour facility. Three boats were tied in the shelter, the largest of which was a modern cruising boat of the sort more usually located in the most exclusive Southern French ports.

With mastery of the sea and the air, Cora Samms' isolation was only geographical. Jack felt he should say something. "You have all that you need here, Miss Samms. Very impressive."

"Yes, we are well provided for. There is no need to leave the island."

"Do you often?"

"Well, my staff, yes, but I never leave the island."

He nodded, then despite himself asked, "Why not?"

She looked at him regally but without trace of annoyance. "Well, Mr McLeod, as you say, I have all that I need here." She added, "I have no other home."

Jack switched to horticultural matters. "This is a fine lawn. I had no idea that this grass would flourish here."

She said, "Alas, Mr McLeod, tons of imported soil, turned and replaced frequently, plus chemicals is the solution."

"And the crops beside the airstrip?"

"The same, I'm afraid. The Isles can bear no crop naturally."

That feature, combined with its location, made the place uninhabitable, unless you had somewhere north of a billion pounds. He stood silently beside her and gazed out to the ocean. No one could feel anything other than small beside this and, for a moment, Jack felt no worse and no better than any other living thing.

She eventually broke off her gaze and turned to him. "Shall we go in?"

He followed her into a modern great hall flanked by a wide marble staircase. She paused, and a few seconds later a dark-haired, dark-featured, slim woman of about forty silently appeared.

Cora Samms said, "Angela, Mr McLeod will freshen up before lunch. Show him to his room." She turned and said, "Will you join me for lunch when you are ready?"

It was a command rhetorically wrapped, and Jack acquiesced

and followed Angela up the staircase.

Chapter 24

Jasper Hunt woke into a late London summer's morning and, for once, was not overcome by a hangover. It was certainly there, for he had polished off most of a bottle of malt last evening, but the effects of the liquor were somehow being overpowered by another feeling which, if he didn't know better, might possibly be happiness.

He could not, of course, be sure; although he had experienced many emotions in a varied life, happiness – real enduring happiness – was an emotion he was not on familiar terms with. Still, whatever it was, it felt good. No need to overanalyse the feeling – let it run and enjoy it.

He got out of bed reasonably freely for a man in his late fifties and instead of heading for coffee and cigarettes, made straight for the shower. He still felt good despite observing the sharp focus the morning light brought to his skin and, with a carefree accompanying song, conducted a vigorous and energising shower. This done, he dressed rapidly and made his way to the kitchen. The table was overflowing with unwashed plates which he brushed aside dismissively to make space for a cup of black coffee and an ashtray.

Hunt had a single important decision to make today and he took it rapidly. Even doctors were allowed to call in sick once in a while and, this call made, he relaxed into his chair and took a deep, satisfying lungful of a cigarette and began to contemplate how he might occupy this, his last free day. Before deciding, he rose from the chair and pulled down a biscuit barrel from a shelf and inspected the contents. Nearly £3,000 at a rough count and that would be about enough for a decent day out in the capital.

As the day was fine, in keeping with his mood, Hunt eschewed the car and walked contentedly in the general direction of the West End. He had a vague idea of purchasing some new clothes, but that could wait, and, armed with his bankroll, he could risk a little on the tables.

A casino was never really at its best around lunchtime and the majority of the clientele cut sorry figures: a couple of ageing and rough-looking women embracing fruit machines, a few Chinese playing roulette, and the whole scene played out to the unmusical accompaniment of vacuum cleaners operated by uninterested cleaners.

Hunt ignored the roulette wheel and sat down on the single, open and unpatronised blackjack table. He changed out five hundred pounds for twenty-five-pound chips, and, without obvious interest, the painted dealer began.

Against the odds, the fall of the cards began to favour Hunt, and in a very short period he was more than a thousand pounds ahead. The dealer suppressed a yawn and showed no concern when Hunt rose and left the table.

He never usually quit when he was ahead, so why had he done so this time? He was never happy, never satisfied and always wanted more. But today he didn't want more, and he left and returned to the busy London street, very soon finding himself entering a small designer menswear shop at the back of Bond Street.

It was empty and, unlike the disinterested croupier, the salesman was highly attentive. Hunt spent the next five minutes reviewing and rejecting the range of garments. Eventually, he settled on a selection of trousers and shirts and repaired to a small fitting room, home to three small, curtained cubicles.

The promise of the garments when displayed failed to translate when decorating Hunt, and he continued to work through them, robing and disrobing with difficulty in the confined space. When removing a particularly ill-fitting pair of trousers, he became aware of someone else entering the fitting room – most terrifyingly and in all probability the over-attentive attendant.

Hunt had no wish to discuss possible purchases without trousers, and he moved quickly and had just about dressed himself as the curtain of the cubicle flew open.

A split-second glance was enough to convince Hunt that it would have been preferable had it been the salesman.

The form which stood only a foot or so from him was massive. Another glance confirmed that Hunt was in extreme danger. He did not have time for a third glance, as the intruder brought a silver object crashing into his temple, which rendered his future plans, at best, on hold.

Chapter 25

Jimmy Trent sat alone in his office and, without focus, shuffled a disarranged collection of letters and documents. They represented the week's sales, leads and enquiries. He noted with concern that the pile was not high. With Ash gone and the partnership dissolved, he had initially supposed that all his business problems would be over. A day on, they were just starting.

A car dealer to the stars with neither clientele nor hope of forging any new connections sounded like an unsustainable business model. He pushed the papers to one side and made a space in front of him on the desk, which he filled with a bottle of vodka and a dirty tumbler. He poured a generous measure of the clear spirit, swallowed a large mouthful and vaguely cogitated on future marketing initiatives. None of them seemed plausible or realistic, and he knew that he would have to think a great deal harder. Three double vodkas later the bottle was exhausted, and so were his ideas.

He lit a cigarette, rocked back on his chair, clicked his computer mouse and conducted a short internet surf, but after finding only marketing and sales advice available at a price he drifted onto a betting site and placed a patriotic bet on a Glasgow Rangers European win. The empty bottle was annoying him now. More alcohol might be the answer. He stubbed out his half-finished cigarette and left his office, making his way past a few sparkling supercars and into a balmy London evening.

He passed a number of fashionable wine bars and their noisy pavement-dwelling customers, but he wasn't in the mood for that sort of thing so opted for the traditional-looking Duke of Clarence public house.

As he entered via the frosted swing doors, he wondered why places like this still existed. At least it was possible to get a seat, and Jimmy had his choice of dozens, except for the two occupied by a couple of old men. He selected a precarious position balanced on a tall, slightly unsteady bar stool. With a smile and an enthusiastic tone, a pleasant girl in her late twenties approached and welcomed him in an Antipodean accent.

He had a lot of thinking to do so he ordered a pint of lager and a double vodka and received a disappointing amount of change. He took a mouthful of the lager and looked again at the girl. Was she Australian or a Kiwi? It always annoyed Antipodeans when you guessed wrong.

"You Australian?"

She looked at him, affected disdain and then slowly shook her head.

Wrong again, Jimmy.

She countered, "You English?"

It served him right. He had another guess. "Are you on holiday?" He missed the mark again.

"No, I've been over here for years. My parents broke with convention and emigrated here."

She was a good-looking girl, worth talking to. He couldn't think of anything to say but she helped him out. "I'm at the art school, the Slade, and I do a few shifts in here."

"What are you studying?"

"I'm a sculptor."

Jimmy said, "Interesting." In truth, she could hardly have chosen a subject that he knew less about, but another look at her pleasant, full face persuaded him to blunder on. "What sort of sculpture?"

She launched into an analysis of the various media of sculpture and described herself as being a great admirer of Lyn Chadwick. "Do you like her?"

He was nodding rhythmically and routinely and only heard her question the second time it was put. He then admitted that he had never heard of Ms Chadwick, and instead offered up Rodin.

She smiled and complimented him faintly. "Most folks can't even name one."

He asked for more drinks. She accepted one for herself and laid a few coins beside a none-too-tall stack at the side of the till and resumed the conversation, mercifully away from sculpture.

"What's your line?" she asked.

"I sell cars."

At last he had found a conversation starter.

"Oh, I'm looking for a new car. I've got an old Corsa and it's starting to let me down. What do you recommend?"

"Well, what sort of budget?"

"A couple of thousand, maybe three at a push. I've been saving for ages."

It was the sort of money that Ash used to snort in a weekend. "Well, the cheapest car I've got is a little bit more expensive than that."

"How much more?"

"I've got an Aston, a few years old, that's been marked down to about £50,000."

Her face fell. "Oh, I see. Well, never mind, you can still advise me. Honestly, I know nothing about cars."

Jimmy knew a bit more than he thought, and after undertaking a superficial review of available budget models, handed her a business card.

She was listening intently. It felt good to be useful.

Throughout, they exchanged smiles. He hadn't had a lover for two years. Celibacy had not been a positive choice. It had just happened, and he supposed that he had gotten used to it. He started to look at the Antipodean sculptress and regarded her in a more primitive way. She was a good-looking girl, but he didn't even know her name.

"I'm Jimmy."

"Karina."

He was out of information on cars so opted for a cautious close. "On second thoughts, I might be able to help you choose a car. If you want?"

"That would be great. I'm off tomorrow, and I was going to go round a few garages."

"I can meet you if you like?"

"Great," she said. "Will I meet you here, say at eleven tomorrow morning?"

Jimmy smiled at her. "Yes, that'll be fine. I was thinking of a day off myself."

He flung down the last of his lager and wished her au revoir, encouraged by having secured what, by an almighty stretch, could be described as a date.

He re-emerged onto the street in decent spirits, buoyed by the turn of events. He had a large amount of cash in his pocket. This wasn't a day for working, so he decided to head west and see what other adventures he could find.

London was about the busiest city in Europe, but two streets from the main thoroughfares was another world. Jimmy ambled through the tree-lined back streets of Kensington, with the distant rumble of traffic now barely audible. Following alongside, a couple of wrens chattered to each other as they darted in and out of a luxuriant rhododendron bush. And then the wrens shut up and there was a complete silence.

It felt, for a split second, like the world had stopped turning and was ready to implode into cosmic oblivion, but the screeching of the tyres of the first black saloon car which stopped ten yards away signalled that mankind was to be spared today.

Jimmy, however, was less lucky, and the three well-built men who emerged from the car clearly were not making a social call.

The man from the offside rear door arrived first and Jimmy knocked him down with a single blow. It was a sweet shot, and the man was out of the contest. At this, the other two moved a pace apart and slowed but didn't halt their advance. They were professionals. Amateurs would have turned tail at the sight of their stricken colleague, but they had a job to do and their faces indicated that they meant to finish.

Two against one wasn't great odds, even for a special forces NCO still in decent shape. The only rule of the martial arts was to avoid confrontation, but avoidance wasn't an option as he registered the sound of more car doors opening from behind him. One thing at a time. The sound of runners behind was getting louder, but there was nowhere to run to, so he focused on what lay ahead. He flicked his eyes between the two men in front. Neither looked obviously weaker.

Both men were stationary two yards away, and about the same distance from each other. He could see their hard, purposeful faces now. He had to close the distance and strike, while not presenting them with an opportunity which both of them looked as if they could take.

His decision was forced when the man on his left took a quick stride forward and aimed a powerful fist at the side of Jimmy's head. A timely reaction rendered the blow glancing only, but it stung his cheekbone and he uttered an involuntary oath.

However, his focus was now acute, and Jimmy brought his heel down on the man's shin. The crunch of breaking bone and the scream of agony told him that a second adversary was disabled. There was only one man between him and flight, but, as he weighed up his final frontal opponent, the footfall from behind became deafening

He had one shot and it had to be now. He took a stride forward, feigned right and delivered left a powerful blow at the man's temple. But the last man anticipated the move and countered effectively with a defensive arm, and in a single slick movement embraced Jimmy in a suffocating clinch which drew the breath from him. He only had seconds before he would pass out. Desperately, he struggled. He freed an arm and prodded a straight finger backwards and flush in his opponent's eye. The suffocating grip immediately relaxed and the man fell howling alongside his colleagues.

There was no time to savour his victory. The path ahead was now clear for flight, and Jimmy's adrenalin-fuelled body felt light and powerful. His stride was long. He covered yards in seconds. He was running like the wind now, exhilarated and safe. Now he could hear nothing from behind, and neither did he feel pain when his vista turned upside down.

Later, he would swear that he heard a note of birdsong as he dived headlong into the bottomless inky black pool.

Chapter 26

Doctor Laura Gibson's mind was a million miles from the task before her. It wasn't a loss of focus, but rather a sharp clarity on a new set of life priorities. Neither work in the conventional sense nor any of the traditional life goals seemed relevant any more. She had crossed a line, and whatever else happened, there was no going back. She signed off the papers in the folder in front of her and left the laboratory, discarding her obligatory white coat for the last time. She had taken the precaution of booking an overdue fortnight's leave, but, as she exited the bland building and got into her bland car, she knew she would never return.

She felt nothing as she drove out of the facility and focused completely on the tasks she still had to close. The house was already sold and financial closure was due imminently, giving her more than enough money for her new life.

And what of the new life? Nothing to worry about. The exact details needed to be filled in, but her general direction was far from vague. She had him and she was going to keep him, whatever the cost. She tossed back her hair assertively and caught a glance of her features in the car's mirror. She looked different today. It was a determined face.

She pulled into her – soon-to-be former – cottage. It was empty now save for a single holdall which sat in the hall.

She took a final walk-through of the cottage. It also felt different today. It had been the centrepiece of her life for fifteen years, but leaving it behind generated neither sentiment nor remorse.

The future was just too powerful, too strong and too desirable, and she exited the cottage without a backward glance and headed off to her solicitors.

The drive took less than five minutes. She was lucky enough to find an adjacent parking space and entered the reception of Snape & Mortimer, Solicitors: a traditional village practice. The office was modern enough, however, and her wait was a short one as Mr Smith, her solicitor, joined her and invited her into his office.

Smith had acted for her for many years, albeit his duties light since managing her initial house purchase. He was about fifty, smoothly spoken and sharply dressed. His office was tidy, and, without small talk, he invited her to sit and then updated her.

"Good news, Doctor Gibson, and good timing. I'm pleased to say we have now closed your sale and the purchaser's funds are in our account." He reached into a nearby folder and extracted a single sheet, which he passed to her. "The statement of account."

She reviewed it rapidly, her eyes alighting on only the bottom-line figure of some £500,000. "Fine."

"Now, to which account would you like the funds transferred?"

"Cash would be best, Mr Smith."

If he was surprised at this, he exhibited no sign. "I can have the cash by tomorrow at noon."

She nodded and, after declining his offer of further legal services, made her way from the solicitor's office, wondering how she would fill in the time until noon tomorrow.

There was nothing in the village and a moment's reflection reminded her she now had no accommodation for the night so, with a vague idea of a night in a nearby hotel, she drove off.

She had been there before, but once out of the village, her sense of direction abandoned her, and she was forced to repeatedly slow at junctions.

This didn't suit other road users. Mostly, the frustrated

motorists overtook quickly, but that wasn't so easy now she was on a narrow part of road and delaying a large black executive saloon car. The car did not noisily protest, but she became increasingly vexed at the frustration she was surely causing its occupants. To her relief, a sign announcing the hotel entrance emerged through the hedgerow, and she indicated and turned into the long entranceway of the country hotel.

The black saloon followed and, from the opposite side of the capacious car park, a happy middle-aged couple emerged. They were totally absorbed with each other and without any interest in remonstrating with her.

The hotel grounds were attractive and in full summer bloom but, inside, the Edwardian hotel smelled musty and the faded reception area was tired.

She was weary now and had no wish to get back into the car, so she booked a so-called superior executive room, paid in advance with cash, and made her way up the stairs.

The door opened easily enough, and she moved in, letting the door close automatically behind her. Only the door did not click behind her. She turned. Framed in the doorway was a dark-featured man. The stranger's suit was well-fitting and his face was impassive. He might have been a hotel employee, but the suit was just too good.

Without words, he moved into the room while she, frozen with fear, could neither move nor utter a sound.

She wasn't sure what happened next, but Laura Gibson, for reasons unknown to her, was soon speeding along country roads in a massive black executive saloon.

Chapter 27

Jack showered in a bathroom as big as a hotel suite and had dressed in casual clothes when Angela Delap knocked on the door. He followed her as they retraced their steps back down to the hall. From there, she led him through a single door to a long bland corridor with doors on each side.

She stopped halfway down the corridor and knocked sharply. This time, she did not enter automatically but waited until a faint sound came from inside. She opened the door and invited him to follow. "Mr McLeod, ma'am," she announced and withdrew.

Custom had not dulled Cora Samms' variety, and the vast room, richly but subtly lit, provided another stunning visual assault. There were no endless, panoramic natural vistas; indeed, there were no windows at all. From every wall hung sumptuously decorated, ceiling-high tapestries depicting scenes from antiquity – some domestic but mostly martial. Vaguely eastern-looking horsemen fought hand to hand in desperate struggle. The artwork was exquisite, and the figures and scenes shimmered life back from their two-dimensional constraints and dominated the cavernous room.

In the centre of the room, Cora Samms sat at a large dining table with two places set. "Please, Mr McLeod, sit down."

He walked to his place, but before sitting he spied another remarkable piece of art. On a plinth at the end of the room stood a fabulous bejewelled model of a horse. It was about three or four feet from extended tail to flared nostril, and its brilliant gold veneer beamed and shimmered out across the room. Jack knew that the gold wouldn't be veneer and, as he vulgarly tried to estimate its weight, was distracted by the greens and reds of the precious stones which served as the teeth and mane of the fabulous beast.

The soft, authoritative voice again invited him to sit. He did so but struggled to remove his gaze from the sublime figure. She didn't interrupt him and, after a moment or so, he recovered his senses and excused himself, mumbling some words of admiration for the fabulous horse.

Her expression was impassive but not unfriendly. "A replica I'm afraid. From the palace of Ctesiphon." She paused and regarded him, as if this explanation would suffice for any moderately learned individual.

Jack admitted his learning did not extend to a working knowledge of the palace of Ctesiphon.

She smiled tolerantly. "A great winter palace of the Persian kings of the seventh century."

He could have done with a bit more background, but they were interrupted by the appearance of James Fay. He cut a towering figure in the full, reddish light.

"Well, Mr McLeod, what would you like to eat?" Cora asked.

There was no menu, but he knew Cora Samms would have everything. He played it safe and challenged Fay with a fillet steak, medium rare, and a small salad.

"Would you like a drink, sir?" Fay asked.

Jack had had enough on the plane. "No, I'm fine with water."

Cora Samms didn't give Fay an order, but he left anyway and returned shortly after with Jack's order, together with a plate of unspecified greens for his mistress.

Jack was unexpectedly hungry and ate as lustily as seemed mannerly while she, from time to time, nibbled at the greens with occasional sips of water. She didn't talk while he ate but the silence wasn't uncomfortable.

When he had finished eating, Fay re-emerged, removed the plates and served coffee.

Samms lit a long cheroot and, following her lead, Jack lit a vulgar cigarette. She leant forward slightly. "I hope you are comfortable. Is there anything else that you need, Mr McLeod?"

"No, thank you. You have a wonderful home. It takes my breath away."

She accepted this assessment, took a deep lungful from the cheroot and returned to the subject of her jewelled horse.

"The Great Kings of Persia, Mr McLeod, they were men of great wisdom and true aesthetes. Fifteen hundred years ago, our rulers introduced us to universal principles which it seems we have largely abandoned today." Her long, grave-featured face transformed to wistfulness. "Tolerance, equity, justness, a love of art and, of course, peace."

Jack nodded involuntarily and she continued. "The great winter palace of Ctesiphon was sumptuous, massive and ornate, but the front was irregularly shaped. When the king was asked why, he replied that this piece of the land was owned by an old woman who had declined to sell at any price and the king would not force her to sell."

With a far-away look in her eyes, she said, "The last days of the Sasarian Empire – splendid indeed, and a thousand years before the European Renaissance."

As he regarded her silently, she stubbed out her cheroot. "Now to art, Mr McLeod." She rose and invited him to follow her as she passed through a gap between the tapestries and opened a large, plain door via a button. This revealed a descending carpeted ramp which they followed, accompanied by low, white lighting which tracked their progress. At the bottom of the ramp, Cora Samms stopped and clapped her hands together. Brilliant white light flooded the entire space to reveal a huge white rectangular room.

Jack's eyes slowly adjusted. He had been amazed so many times in one day, but as his eyes scanned the artworks, he prepared for what he knew would be the most incredible experience to date.

"This way, Mr McLeod." She beckoned him to follow as they embarked upon what would hopefully be a long, deep and systematic viewing of what already looked to have been accurately billed as the greatest private art collection in history.

Chapter 28

Most art collections had a bias of some sort. Some were geographical, some covered periods in history, and some were associated with art movements and styles. But not the collection of Cora Samms. Renaissance, Baroque, Romantic, eighteenth, nineteenth and twentieth century together for comprehensive coverage of the history of Western art. One criterion only was applied, apparently: whatever period, the art must be the best.

Jack's senses were reeling. He didn't know where to start and he didn't know what to say. He looked at his hostess. He could not imagine her feelings.

Her face betrayed neither pride nor hubris. "Shall I show you around, Mr McLeod, or would you like to browse alone?"

There could be only one answer. Whatever Cora Samms was, or might turn out to be, this was her collection and she was part of it. The thoughts of the curator were an indivisible and essential part of any viewing experience; besides which, Amanda would doubtless recommend spending the maximum possible time with the target. "If you have the time, I'd love you to show me."

She nodded and began the tour. Her rich voice was mesmeric. She recommended his attention to the first exhibit, a Renaissance oil. "The young Raphael. A contemporary of Leonardo and Michelangelo and alongside – can you guess?"

Jack reviewed a small, poetic scene of spectacular colour. He shuffled some names around in his head and then managed a shot in the dark. Giorgione was one of the key founders of the High Renaissance, although very little was known about him and very few pictures were attributed to him.

Cora Samms seemed impressed. "Very good, Mr McLeod."

There followed a whirlwind tour of a dozen or so other Venetian masterpieces showcasing Titian, Veronese and Tintoretto. Jack, however, had no time to dwell on these for, hanging alone, was a coveted favourite. If he had been anywhere else it would have been a print or a fake, and, as he was not standing in the Prado, he had not expected to see what was undeniably a view of Toledo, Spain – certainly at the very least in the style of El Greco. Whosoever was the pupil or apprentice, he had learned well, and the massive impasto oil was stunning. It was one of his favourite paintings. Jack had visited the original only a few years before, so it was very well known to him.

Cora Samms must have read his thoughts. "The Greek painted more than one scene of the city. I think this is the equal of the example in Spain."

Jack pushed his face nearer the work. "I agree."

Before he was ready, she walked on and conducted a rapid review of a selection of Impressionist and Modern works, mercifully not including Gauguin, moved on to Modigliani and then halted at a section devoted to Picasso. If the number of works in the collection was any guide, it appeared that the Spanish master was Cora's favourite. Amanda had chosen her bait well.

There were numerous examples from the Blue and Rose Periods, ventures into cubism and even a few spectacular ceramics.

"How do you like Picasso, Mr McLeod?"

"A good deal, but perhaps not as much as you?"

"Yes, he may be my favourite," she admitted.

Jack had an admission of his own. "Of course, usually his best works are a bit out of my league." Not that she knew what his league was, of course.

"Well, if you sell me your picture, it would enable you to, as they say, be promoted a league."

This footballing metaphor sounded very odd on her lips. He smiled and said wistfully, "Yes, maybe, but I haven't agreed to sell. Well, perhaps not yet."

This qualifier seemed to please her. "Mr McLeod, you know that I am keen, more than keen, to acquire your painting. Mr Fay offered you $125 million, which you did not accept. I am prepared to increase this offer to $200 million, payable immediately to any bank account in the world."

Jack said nothing. It was a lot of money. He had to remind himself he was not authorised to sell.

"I am aware that there exists a possibility," she said, "that in a competitive auction it may realise even more. It is, to our knowledge, a unique example."

That amount of money deserved an immediate reply. "Well, Miss Samms, I am of course quite comfortably off at present."

She flashed him a wintery smile, making him feel like a pauper.

"Owning a work like this is an impossible dream, the Holy Grail. For me, a once in a lifetime opportunity to own something truly unique, and something desired by many. I am, after all, also an art collector."

It wasn't a bad speech by his standards.

"Of course, I understand this. However, even for me, my desire sometimes exceeds my reach. There is the question of maintenance and, of course, the security issues associated with owning such a work."

She wasn't threatening to steal it herself, although Jack couldn't be completely sure, so he nodded in agreement with these practical assessments.

"I think, under the circumstances, I can offer the work the perfect home."

"It would certainly sit very well here," Jack said.

"Excuse me a moment, Mr McLeod."

Samms walked towards a curtained area at the end of the room and returned with what looked like a decent example of a work by a Scottish colourist. She held it alongside a Picasso oil about as big as a door. "Do you see the difference, Mr McLeod?"

About a day ago, Jack would have raved over the Scottish work, but now it looked derivative, and it was overshadowed by its neighbour.

"Ah, you see it," she said softly.

He did. His own extensive but more modestly priced collection, carefully curated over the years, could, if juxtaposed with the Picasso, never again be enjoyed by him in the same way. At a stroke, the collection would seem inferior, inadequate, and he might grow to despise it. And what could he buy, thereafter, to sit alongside it? It was a bleak outcome: collections, any collections, should be built up and improved gradually over years.

Amanda's picture did, as Cora Samms asserted, belong here.

"Now, why don't I leave you to browse at your own pace, Mr McLeod?"

"Yes, thank you."

Samms disappeared through a well-disguised door at the far end of the gallery, with an instruction that, should he need assistance, a large white button on the walls should be pressed.

Once alone, Jack exhaled loudly. He was playing a dangerous game. Samms had all the power and influence in the world and her retainers – at least the three he had met so far – looked like some of the most dangerous individuals he had ever encountered. At minimum, she would react badly to her time being wasted. At worst, given Amanda's interest, God knows.

He could do nothing about this now, so he composed himself and slowly continued with the show, noting with enthusiasm more modern works by Hockney, Bacon, Kirchner, Beckman and Hopper, as well as a full representation from the Baroque masters Vermeer, Reubens and Rembrandt.

Her tastes were not miles away from his own. Perhaps the

world's greatest private collection had no place for Klimt, Pollock, Warhol or any equivalent uninspiring over-hyped daubings.

In the middle of the vast space, she had a version of Böcklin's Isle of the Dead, and he was immediately struck by an obvious analogy to Samms' own universe. A long, ice-cold shiver ran from the base of his skull to the small of his back. Just how far would this analogy stretch?

Chapter 29

After an hour, although Jack was far from finished with the collection, he was ready to leave, and he pressed one of the wall-mounted buttons. From somewhere, another of Samms' retainers appeared before him. Like James Fay, the man was tall and powerful, his features impassive with a hint of menace. This was the man who had driven Jack to the airport and had, probably, piloted the plane.

Jack was able to observe him more closely. He bore an uncanny resemblance to Angela Delap, and Jack marked them down as related.

"I'd like to walk in the grounds if that is okay?"

The man nodded. "Certainly, sir. Would you like a tour or will you please yourself?"

"I don't want to trouble anyone."

"Of course, sir. This way."

He led Jack through the door which Samms had used earlier to a bland, neutrally decorated corridor and a short flight of stairs which returned him to the ground-floor reception area.

The retainer enquired obsequiously whether Jack needed anything else and, receiving a reply in the negative, left him to his own devices.

He glanced at his watch. It was not yet five, so he had a good hour to amble without purpose and gather information for

Amanda.

He went out the front door and re-emerged onto the extensive lawns which rolled unbroken and unbounded to some distant rocks, presumably marking its extent. Jack ambled towards the rocks, a walk of about a hundred yards and, sure enough, when he arrived at the rocks, it was clear they marked the boundary of the lawns. Beyond, the ground gave way precipitously to nothingness. He edged forward gingerly. The drop was sheer – must be three or four hundred feet down to the North Atlantic Ocean. A second or two looking down was all he could manage.

He inched back from the unguarded edge to the safety of the lawns and walked to the head of the metalled road above the harbour. He descended. The design would win no awards, but as he wandered along one of the protruding crude concrete legs, he realised that the construction represented a major engineering achievement. The navigation through the defending rocky outlets would have been tricky even before embarking upon whatever foundations were necessary to hold a structure in a thousand feet of Atlantic Ocean. Whatever the design, the whole thing was a triumph, and the ability to receive good-sized ships would have transformed the prospects for living in this remote spot.

The concrete gangway was lined with tall sturdy regularly spaced metal poles which provided lighting. Every other pole was topped with what looked like a camera. No chances were taken with security, even here. There was nothing else to see, so he retraced his steps back up the road, this time bypassing the lawn.

Near the head of the wide road and on the opposite side to the house, the lines of crops began, punctuated only by two huge corrugated hangar-like constructions. The road ended when it met the final length of the runway and, as he had already surveyed the length of the airstrip, he proceeded behind the house where James Fay had earlier driven the golf buggy.

He passed four small terraced cottages and miscellaneous stone-built outbuildings. He could not be sure of their exact purpose –

certainly domestic in character, but the living arrangements were unclear, as was the exact number of servants on the island. He had counted only three staff so far, which seemed light for the establishment.

He wanted a closer look at one of the cottages and moved a few steps from the road to peer through one of the low windows. He managed only one step before Angela Delap emerged from one of the buildings. She looked reasonably welcoming and said, "Can I help you with something, Mr McLeod?"

"No, not really," he said with a nonchalant air. "I'm just having a walk."

"Shall I join you?" It seemed a more appealing prospect than a promenade with her brother, so Jack accepted.

She joined him on the road. "Down?"

Jack nodded, and they continued along the road, not as steep as on the other side of the island, until they were clear of the buildings, whereupon the land began to fall a little faster. The sister island, Lessor, rose steeply ahead of them. They continued down the road without speaking.

On the highest point of Lessor, Jack observed the tops of what seemed like a collection of Nissen huts.

He broke the silence and asked what they were.

"Oh, army buildings."

He was here as a vendor of art, so it seemed all right to enquire further. "Army – what do they do out here?"

She smiled pleasantly. "You know, I'm really not sure. We never go over there."

Jack had thought of the Isles of Grace as a single mass, but as they descended further, he saw that this was not so. Although the land masses were close, they were fully separated by a precipitous narrow ravine.

They continued along the road until they came to a crude pontoon bridge. It seemed well dug into either side of the ravine, but the entire construction was swaying from what was surely, for these parts, only a moderate wind.

The metalled road continued beyond the bridge and up the slopes of Lessor. It was wide enough for vehicles, although it looked a tough incline.

The bridge was guarded by a closed metal padlocked gate.

Jack edged a pace or two forward and looked down. The view was terrifying. The islets were separated by no more than the length of the bridge. Hundreds of feet below, the part of the ocean pressured into the narrow strait boiled and raged in protest. He took a step backwards.

"End of the road," Angela said, and he nodded. He had a last look down at the boiling ocean and then turned back. As they retraced their steps, he observed the dismal natural state of the uncultivated island: a mixture of rock with some rough grass and scrub.

Angela was a woman of few words and Jack didn't feel the need to talk. She escorted him back as far as the last cottage, whereupon she left him, and he made his way back to the front lawns, where he stood for some time, staring out to sea.

He looked at the long wild grasses that bounded the lawn. Something was missing. There was no drone from an industrious bee; not even a pesky wasp to swat away. The ocean occasionally roared from down below, but for a moment it took a break. The wind fell and no seabirds broke the skyline. He shut his eyes and experienced, for the first time in his life, total silence. Maybe that's what death felt like.

Chapter 30

Enjoying a long, hot bath as part of his preparation for dinner then departure, Jack reflected on what exactly he had learned about Cora Samms and her establishment.

She was well bred, faultless as a hostess and passionate about fine art. Her household consisted of at least three staff and that was about it. Surely MI5 could have dug up that much themselves, especially as the army was camped about a mile away. The army and that base worried him. If Amanda was interested in Samms, her interest would be far from trivial, and with a top-secret army base so near, the possibilities horrific.

Jack shrugged that aside, washed his face roughly and emerged from the tub refreshed. It was a quarter to seven now and he must dress; he knew that Angela Delap would summon him exactly on time. He dressed quickly and hurriedly packed his bag to be ready for an immediate departure. Sure enough, the knock came at the appointed time and he followed her down the stairs to the dining room, leaving his bag in the hall.

To his surprise, he was greeted by the sight of not only his hostess but three men in army dress uniform. Fuck, did Amanda know everything?

Cora Samms did the honours. "I thought you might tire of my company. These are our neighbours, Mr McLeod. Colonel Braid, the commanding officer, and Captains Harris and Johnston."

Jack shook all of them by the hand and managed a smile of sorts. This was an opportunity lost to discuss art. Amanda probably wouldn't have agreed, though.

Braid looked uneasy, and clearly Johnston didn't want to be there. Harris only just managed to mask a perceptible yawn with a false-sounding laugh. It looked like these dining engagements were more of a duty than a pleasure.

Cora Samms indicated the dining table. "Shall we sit, gentlemen?"

They did. Fay came in and outlined a few menu options and they all ordered. Jack had a drink this time, as did everyone else bar Cora, who stuck to water.

Braid was the one to break the ice. He said, "So, Mr McLeod, how are things on the mainland?"

"Oh, much the same," Jack replied blandly. "Economic uncertainty, wars in the Middle East, raging political correctness."

Fay had returned with food as he spoke and Braid was now a lot more interested in his rib of beef than Jack's answer.

He finished chewing – almost – and said, "The country needs a lot of changes. Too much public spending. Taxes too high."

In a former life, Jack had been employed as an Economics lecturer. He could discuss this all night – but he didn't want to. Luckily, he didn't need to. The younger and taller of the two captains, Simon Johnston, weighed in.

"Whole country's gone flabby. I mean, look at the armed forces. Tiny these days. Makes you wonder, if there was another war what we would do? Would people fight for their country?"

At this, Cora Samms interposed. "What of those that do not have a country, Captain Johnston?"

Damn the soldiers for being there – it could have provided a promising opening for further enquiry, but the opportunity disappeared as quickly as it had appeared when Johnston ignored the question and moved on to the flabbiness of the criminal justice system.

Jack actually agreed with some of what Johnston was saying, but he drew the line at agreeing with someone as downright annoying as Johnston so, at least publicly, he withheld his support.

Throughout all this, Harris had not uttered a word. He was bored and he had the class to show it.

Jack sought to broaden the discussion with some mundane chat. "What kind of facilities have you got on the island? Satellite TV?"

Harris spoke for the first time. "Afraid not. No football."

Braid jumped in and added, "And worse than that, yesterday the radio equipment at the base broke down."

"The parts will be here in a day or so," Johnston said. "Really we are quite well served." He looked at Cora. "And we have very hospitable neighbours."

She nodded in acknowledgement. Jack caught Harris rolling his eyes.

The conversation was poor but at least the food was good, again served by the multi-talented James Fay. Desultory and bland conversation continued as they enjoyed sweets and cheese and then it was brandy.

Four of the five guests began to smoke. Harris and Johnston headed for the French windows. Surprisingly, Samms rose and followed them.

Jack was alone with Braid, and he put the time to good use.

Chapter 31

It was nearly midnight when Jack returned to the Grange Hotel. He could have been earlier, but he had insisted on being dropped at the Park Lane hotel and gave it forty-five tedious minutes before skulking out the back. It wasn't much of a subterfuge. Cora Samms could influence governments, so she could presumably locate Jack in an emergency, but it made him feel better.

Customer service at the Grange for once fell short of its usual standards and a young male receptionist with ill-fitting uniform seemed to be, at first sight, sleeping. He was conscious, though, and shambled to attention just before Jack got to the desk bell.

He had his room key with him but, after the surreal trials of the last twenty-four hours, was in desperate need of room service. After a short exchange, the man disappeared for a moment or two before returning with a bottle of bourbon, a bucket of ice and a large tumbler. Jack scrawled on a crude receipt, gave the man ten pounds for his trouble and struggled with the tray into the glass elevator.

Back in his room, he laid the tray on a small table and flung open the narrow French windows, which led to a small balcony. The night was fine, and he poured a long drink and moved outside and into the cool of the London air. He took a long mouthful of the burning bourbon. It would be some time before he could sleep, so he didn't try. His mind raced between thoughts of Cora Samms, her art collection, her sinister retainers but, most of all, Braid's desperate and risky plea for help, which was all he had managed in the thirty seconds they had had together.

A glance at Braid had convinced Jack that his terror was real, and it was so acute that it could only be terror for his life. Who and what was Braid afraid of? And did Braid himself even know? The pool of suspects was narrow, but that didn't help, for the pool was full of sharks and for Braid, in mortal fear and confined to his outpost, things must be unbearable.

Jack's mind drifted on to Samms, principally her art collection. He swore. That was the least the collection deserved but he found his mind alternating from wonder to disgust.

The value of the collection was billions of pounds. He was struggling to balance the right of personal freedom with wealth inequalities. A stunning and beautiful collection; but to hide it away for selfish pleasure, to have all that just for yourself, was almost sinful.

Cora Samms was a flawless hostess with impeccable manners, but now Jack was at a distance, her other features dominated. She was single-minded, selfish and passionate. As an image of her granite greying features came into his head, he knew that he had never met a more dangerous individual. A third tumbler of bourbon was about all he could manage, and he staggered inside and fell on top of the bed.

His eyes clicked shut. He thought about Amanda. Her briefing had been, by any measure, inadequate, but then her blue eyes appeared and, in his mind, she was smiling at him. He fell asleep.

Chapter 32

When a man was hungover, exhausted and nearly forty years old, he needed more than five hours' sleep, but when Jack checked his phone, it was five a.m. Maybe it was five p.m.? His aching body and thumping head said not.

There was another person in his room.

Jack rubbed his eyes and he was, mostly, relieved to find that it was Amanda. He had texted her the previous evening to tell her of his return. She, in turn, had said she would call the next morning, and now she was sitting on the edge of his bed.

"For fuck's sake, it's five in the morning!" he said.

"Yes."

He grunted then buried his head far under the duvet. He felt the bed give a little as she got off, and then heard the kettle being filled and coming to the boil. There followed the unmistakeable sound of curtains being drawn, then windows being opened. Jack knew it was only a matter of time, so he retreated further within the duvet as she marched around, moving glasses, bottles, clothes and other miscellaneous debris. This done, he heard the crash of a glass on the bedside table.

Amanda resumed her seat on the bed. The duvet did its job blocking her telepathic promptings, so she thrust her hand under the duvet, for no more than a second or two. The sensation of her touch on his thigh woke him up more than any verbal promptings.

It also reminded him he was a man, so he stuck his head out of the duvet and said heroically, "Why don't you get in here if you want to discuss things?"

As an experienced, attractive, single woman, it was possible that Amanda had received worse offers, but when he reflected on it afterwards, it was hard to think what they might be.

Without much consideration she declined this resistible offer, not verbally but by the expedient of rising and walking to the French windows, taking the duvet with her. She said sweetly, "Get up and into the shower, you lazy bastard, we've work to do."

He tried to tough it out for a moment or two, but after not much more than a few seconds, God's gift to womanhood – naked – shuffled past her indifferent glance and did as he was told.

He moaned pitifully in response to a shock of hot water. And then it felt good. But even this couldn't be undertaken in private, for a moment later the door opened. Amanda turned down the toilet lid and sat.

As Jack was unable to speak, she began. "Right, I promised you an update. As I mentioned the other day, I'm investigating a murder." He grunted and she continued. "A car salesman near King's Cross."

Jack started with a few incomprehensible words from his water-filled mouth, and then he got his act together. "Yes, go on. You told me that, and you told me that you were interested in this army base."

"I'm not sure yet of all the facts, but, in simple terms, there is some top-secret work going on there and it involves some pretty dangerous material. I'm not sure exactly what it is or its exact application but for discussion purposes let's say it's enriched plutonium or something like that. Put simply, some of it is unaccounted for, missing."

Jack was as bad a physicist as Amanda, but he groaned. "For Christ's sake. Isn't that the stuff that goes in nuclear bombs?"

"Yes, it is dangerous," Amanda admitted.

Jack had woken up now. "Dangerous to the extent that, in the wrong hands, it can level cities and kill millions?"

She didn't answer.

He kept up the offensive. "Fuck, can't you people keep anything safe?"

"It would seem not."

On behalf of humanity he cursed again and said, "Well, careless as you lot are, I expect with something this serious the solution is obvious?"

Amanda didn't seem to think so.

"Get on to the army brass, send over some marines or something and get it stopped."

She considered this sophisticated plan for a moment. "Well, we could do that, but there are a few issues with your approach. Firstly – and this is the good news – we are fairly sure that nothing has yet left the island."

"How do you know that?"

"The discrepancies arose only a week or so ago and, of course, we are able to comprehensively monitor all naval traffic from the island."

Jack said, reasonably intelligently, "But Samms has a jet, the stuff could have been flown anywhere in the world."

"No, we can monitor all flights also."

"I doubt that – if you are stupid enough to lose the stuff once, I'm sure you can contrive to lose it twice."

Amanda ignored this criticism and continued, "So maybe it's something that we can manage without risking publicity."

"Yes, okay, fine, so get over to the island and shut it down, quietly. For Christ's sake, it's in the middle of the Atlantic. How quiet do you need?"

She smiled at him. "Well, we could, but surely you can see that, if I'm right, there is the question of potential involvement of at least some senior serving army personnel, possibly both on and off the island. Maybe even Cora Samms. We need to find out the extent of any conspiracy."

Jack tried again. "Well, just kick out Samms, sack all the staff and look for the missing material."

"And where do the sackings stop – on the island, in Whitehall?" And then she added, "In any event, it would seem that matters are soon to come to a head – the radio's broken and Braid's pleading for help."

"If the radio's broken, why didn't Braid use Samms' radio?"

She answered the question with a very obvious answer. "Clearly Braid doesn't trust Samms."

"What about satellite phones or something. Surely they don't just rely on a single radio for communications?"

"Yes, I agree, I thought they would have those."

This started to sound faintly less fantastic and he added, "And why did Braid not confide in his boss?" The answer to this question was the same as to the last one.

He had woken up a bit now. "Oh, I forgot to mention, Braid was at dinner last night."

"You fucking tell me that now?"

"Sorry, Samms invited the base officers over for dinner. Think it was a monthly thing."

"Okay, I'm listening."

"Well, it was just dinner. Braid was there with his deputies: two captains, Harris and Johnston. Not much of an atmosphere. None of them wanted to be there, to be honest. But I did get a chance to speak to Braid. Just for a moment."

"Did you mention Andrew Baxter?"

"Yes, I had about thirty seconds alone with him. All he said was 'Tell Andrew I need help'."

"That's all?"

"There was no more time. It was just before I left on the plane."

Amanda wasn't saying anything so Jack said, "Okay, I give up. What are you going to do?"

"Well, someone needs to get over there to help Braid regain

control, in a discreet way at first and preferably without Samms' knowledge. And take it from there. Remember – this is a facility that shouldn't be there. If Samms is not involved, we want to regain control and continue. This sort of research needs to go on, and if not there, then where?"

Jack turned off the shower and she threw him a towel, whereupon he moved back through to the room, lit a cigarette and moved out onto the small balcony. Amanda joined him.

Jack said, "Good, well, you seem to know what you're doing. Am I off the hook? What do I do about the picture?"

Amanda didn't answer at first and he said again, "Well, what now?" She still didn't answer, and he turned towards her enquiringly. He wasn't alarmed at this stage, but a glance at her expression raised a wild thought. He expunged it as quickly as it had formed, by which time she started to talk.

"As to the picture – well, let's play for a bit more time. Say you need a couple more days, maybe a week."

"Okay," he said slowly.

She continued, "As to 'off the hook', not quite yet." She was talking slowly and, it seemed to him, choosing her words very carefully, inevitably working up to asking another favour. "As I say, we need to make a discreet landing and get control of the facility."

Jack heard only the word "we" and took a lungful of smoke and laughed artificially loudly. "We? We? Surely the wrong pronoun, Amanda?" Yet as he said it, he knew that she had not made a mistake. He said, this time without a trace of laughter and a rising sense of alarm, "Christ, Amanda, you are joking, surely? Take the army, marines, SAS, anyone – you can't need me?"

"Well, it might be that I could find someone else that I can completely trust, but only a very small landing can succeed and, besides, you are about the only person I know that I can trust and who knows the island."

His mind conjured up images of the various strong, dangerous men on the island. "Yes, I've been there for about half a day or so

– hardly counts as knowing the layout. Surely there's someone else?"

"Not that I know, and certainly no one who is available to go now."

Jack swore again. He lit another cigarette. "I'm too old, too fat, and I'm too scared."

She shrugged. "Maybe."

Out of energy to protest, he said, "And how do we get there – helicopter or something?"

"Out of the question – a helicopter would alert both base personnel and Samms."

Good – he didn't like helicopters. A split-second later, however, he considered the alternatives. He didn't like boats either. "So, a boat, then?"

"Well, certainly a marine expedition seems indicated."

This was a curious form of words and Jack looked at her carefully.

"And this is where you come in. Tell me all about the island."

He gave her the bad news. Despite the spacious harbour on Main, there could be no prospect of sailing into it and avoiding the harbour cameras. He told her of the precipitous slopes which surrounded the island, at least as far as he had seen, and described the endless depth of the abyss separating the two islets. He could make no suggestion as to where, and even if, a covert marine landing was possible.

Amanda furrowed her brow for a moment before deciding on a short phone call and an equally short conference with an unknown party.

"Right, get dressed, we need to go."

He did so mechanically – he was on an inevitable course – and, less than five minutes later, they got into a taxi on the way to God knows where.

Chapter 33

Their destination wasn't a secret for long. After a short taxi journey, Jack and Amanda were deposited in an upmarket part of town at the edge of the West End. It was mostly residential, although a few commercial offices advertised their services from some of the upper windows.

Jack followed Amanda a little way along the street and up a few steps, whereupon she buzzed an intercom, which released a heavy paint-flaked door.

The inner building was equally nondescript, and beyond a slender glass door, a few steps led to a traditional staircase within a bland hall.

Amanda went into a ground floor room and it was only a minute or so before she returned and led Jack up the uncarpeted stairs, which, in turn, led to a similarly undecorated upper landing with four unmarked doors.

Amanda knocked on one of them.

"Come in," a voice roared.

They entered a large, highly furnished office. Its bay window marked it out as either the Edwardian sitting room or, if from a later period, the master bedroom. The room was carpeted and consisted of a desk topped with modern accessories and with enough room for a low, circular table surrounded by chairs.

Sitting behind the desk was a man. He indicated to them to sit, which they did, and, without speaking, he rose from behind the desk and joined them at the table.

He was a fine-looking man in his late fifties – the kind of man who oozed power and looked good doing it. His hair was still mostly dark and his suit fitted his tall form perfectly.

A moment or so passed in silence.

This silence wasn't broken by any of the three present, but by an efficient-looking woman who entered bearing tea.

This poured, Amanda said, "This is Jack Edwards, and Jack, this is my boss, Andrew Baxter." The men looked at each other and shook hands.

Baxter said, in a surprisingly broad Scottish accent, "Nice to meet you, Mr Edwards. I've heard quite a bit about you. You have quite a taste for adventure."

Jack sipped on his tea. His was the more refined Scottish accent and he wielded it without shame. "Not at all. In fact, I'm bloody sick of it. Why can't you people sort out your own messes and leave us amateurs alone?"

Baxter nodded. "Yes, I quite agree with you, Mr Edwards." He added soothingly, "It's good that you haven't a taste for this sort of stuff. As you say, amateurs are a problem, especially enthusiastic amateurs. Anyway, thanks for agreeing to help us out."

Having not even applied, the interview was over and Jack had got the job.

Baxter's gaze alighted on Amanda. "What have you got?"

She spoke for about fifteen minutes, re-telling pretty much the discussion they had conducted earlier. Baxter did not interrupt and, when she had finished, made no immediate comment.

"I'm not sure, Amanda," he said eventually. "Christ, it's risky. Army intelligence, MI5 and MI6, all of them have probably got an interest. If you fail, or we're wrong, they'll crap on us from a great height."

It was a beautiful metaphor, entirely appropriate.

Amanda said, "I agree, but I can see no other way. We have a duty to Braid."

She exchanged a glance with Baxter, which Jack analysed as an acknowledgement that this alone was of no importance in the grand scheme of things. Braid was expendable and, for that matter, so was everyone else.

Amanda continued, "However, we are faced with the likelihood of the loss of this material, and I don't see how we can sit back and allow that to happen. Samms is either in it or not. I think she is, and as for the officers and others in our facility, an insider is indicated. We need to intervene but who can we look to and trust?" She ended with what sounded almost like a call to arms. "We must act, and we must act alone." She stared her boss down. "Do you trust Braid?"

He considered and nodded.

Jack decided to intervene and heard himself offering the opinion that Braid had seemed genuinely terrified. It was a pretty stupid statement, which only served to make the crazy venture seem more necessary. As neither he nor Amanda had anything else left to say, the – by now customary – period of silence ensued before Baxter spoke.

"What do you need?"

Before Amanda replied, she asked, "How much deniability?"

More like how much – or rather how little – support they could expect in the event of any failure.

He answered more honestly than reassuringly. "Depends how big a failure, Amanda. I'll stand for as much as I can."

Jack had no idea how trustworthy Amanda's boss was or how far he would go. However, Amanda seemed satisfied. "Jack, there are potential outcomes which might leave us, even if we live, rather hung out to dry."

Well, that was one way of putting it. "Likely" should be substituted for "potential", but he agreed with Amanda's assessment. No glory if successful, and death or worse if not.

Jack had one more question. "We believe an amount of this material has been or will be stolen. We do not know by whom. Let me ask. If this stuff is lost, how much damage could be done?"

If a man was to risk his life, Baxter evidently believed he had a right to know what for. "It isn't just the material; it's the means of delivery that's critical. Imagine, if you will, a feasible nuclear bomb the size of a cigarette pack which can be simply transported and detonated. A terrorist with just one device could level Beijing or Paris. Actually, we believe each bomb is roughly equal to about three or four hundred Hiroshimas."

Jack didn't care much for the Chinese or the French but he didn't wish that on them. Unsaid but equally likely were London, Edinburgh or Belfast, and that really frightened him. He shut his eyes and nodded to Baxter and then to Amanda. He was in.

Amanda returned to Baxter's earlier question. "We need to get there, unseen by the navy. Then we need to find a way to land. Finally, we need some stuff."

Were those requests in descending order of difficulty? "Stuff", which Jack took to mean guns, could be sourced.

"I've made a few calls," Baxter said, "and as to getting there, I may have a way. Obviously, we need a vessel which has a legitimate reason to be in the area. I've found one – a supply ship, works on contract for the Royal Navy. Its normal route takes it about two or three miles from the islands and I think would suit us." He pushed a couple of teacups aside and produced a maritime map, which he spread across the table.

His finger traced a path from somewhere on the west coast of England, past the top of Northern Ireland and then vaguely north. His finger stopped and he used another to illustrate a very short distance to a small outcrop of land. "I think this is a communication and satellite black spot, so you'll be invisible. I've advised the skipper of the precise spot. We can trust him."

How Baxter had gained the skipper's confidence hardly seemed to matter.

Amanda nodded keenly. "When do we go?"

"Leave Liverpool at eight o'clock tonight."

Jack was way ahead of them now and was already feeling vaguely seasick. It wouldn't be a luxury yacht and that was bad, but not nearly as bad as the vessel which would likely attempt to deliver them the last few miles.

Amanda seemed unconcerned. "Now, as to the landing, we're not really sure about the lie of the land."

This was another classic understatement, but Amanda's boss was again up to the task. He rose, went to his desk and returned with a huge cloth map which, although worn and faded, seemed admirable for the purpose. It turned out to be on a scale of one to 50,000, and although the charting was about a hundred years old, it did cover the Isles of Grace.

Baxter pointed out the key features with an extended finger. "This is Main, I think it's called. That's where Samms lives and, over here, Lessor, which is where you land. An approach from the north is out of the question, so it has to be south. As you can see, the cliffs seem continuous, save for here."

Jack strained at the map. There was a small break in the tight contour lines, but the map was not small enough scale to allow any degree of confidence.

Baxter admitted as much. "Well, it's not completely clear if it's suitable for an amphibious landing, but it looks the best bet."

When compared to the other unknowns, this hardly seemed to matter, and after a further assessment of the island's topography, it became clear that there was no other possibility.

The meeting was over, and the mission decided. Baxter rose, folded the map and handed it to Amanda. He then shook both their hands and returned behind his desk.

Amanda led Jack out of the office and back to the hall. This time, she selected a door which led to a set of stairs leading down into what seemed like a general storage area, shelved from floor to ceiling. In the centre was a large battered pine table with a chair alongside, occupied by the same lady who had earlier supplied the tea. She showed no surprise at their entrance, and she and Amanda started shopping.

First, a couple of old-looking but robust canvas holdalls were produced. In the first of these, they quickly began loading sealed packets of dried foods and miscellaneous survival aids.

The woman then unlocked a cabinet on the wall and went back and forward with two assault weapons, two shotguns, and then packets of ammunition. Amanda dealt with the handguns. She turned to Jack and presented one handgun to him, then another.

"Browning or Glock?" He shrugged so she decided for him and despatched four of the Brownings into the bag, which was sealed after a metal box, rather like that used for eggs, was included.

Jack became aware of the two women staring at him.

"Large," said Amanda, but the "extra-large" assessment of the other woman carried the day and a plastic-covered overall, a sort of wet or dry suit, was flung onto the table, followed by another, probably better-fitting, garment for Amanda.

Rather than guess, they asked Jack his shoe size, and he was rewarded with a pair of high, part-laced boots. They looked uncomfortable.

This done, Amanda signed a document carelessly and invited Jack to take the suits and the lighter of the two holdalls. She took the other and he followed her out of the house.

Chapter 34

This time they had no need of a taxi. From a long black saloon parked opposite emerged a fresh-faced, powerfully built man who addressed Amanda as "Ma'am". He opened the boot, into which their bags were deposited. The young man returned to the driver's seat and Jack and Amanda sat in the back. She lit two cigarettes, passing one to him. He looked at his watch. It was not yet eight but he had been up for two hours. He was hungry.

"What about something to eat?"

She considered. "Yes, why not? We've a long day ahead."

And night and the next day.

Amanda issued an instruction and the car purred off through the heavy London traffic, until it turned up a small lane which widened at its end and contained an old-style breakfast grill establishment.

"Stay with the car, Peter," Amanda said. "I'll send something out."

They entered the grill and in an instant Amanda was received by a large, overweight, red-faced man – a typical London geezer. He greeted Amanda with affection and respect and quickly found them a booth at the rear of the building, set a little apart from the others. "Send out a couple of bacon rolls and tea to Peter, please," she said. He nodded and left.

"Friend of yours?"

"We go back a long way – professionally, of course."

The high-class service continued and they both enjoyed a satisfying fry-up. She was obviously also hungry and spoke little until they were both replete.

"What's the plan now?" he asked. "Can I go back to bed?"

"Some sleep would be a good idea, but we need to get to Liverpool, and we have a bit to do first."

He was too tired to ask what and he followed her back to the car.

This time Amanda sat in the front seat and immediately reached for a radio. "This is Groucho. Are all cars in position?"

Voices declaring themselves as Chico, Harpo and Gummo responded in the affirmative. "Go!" Jack grabbed the handle as their driver floored it. Peter beat the traffic by use of a siren and wove through the Central London roads until they reached Trafalgar Square and then off the main road, screeching to a halt in a back street just behind Charing Cross station.

The intercom crackled again, and a voice came through clearly. "Target off train, estimated contact time two minutes." The small lane was deserted but for a few late commuters. Telling Jack to wait in the car, Amanda and Peter got out of the car – he going down the lane and she waiting at its head.

Jack was sufficiently familiar with Amanda's activities to recognise that danger was involved as, although neither visible nor drawn, she was clearly handling a firearm under her well-fitting suit. A second later, she released her hand from the gun and moved to partially support the either dead or at least unconscious figure Peter was roughly handling and moving towards the car.

A moment later, they bundled the heavy, middle-aged man into the back seat beside Jack, and in a further instant the car had turned and, again with sirens blaring, sped off down the Mall.

The unconscious man was sprawled over Jack but, after a short struggle, Jack managed to sit him upright and hold him in position. Peter raced past the palace, past Victoria and then screeched into an underground car park. There were plenty of spaces and the car raced to the end of the level and stopped alongside a heavy red safety door. With perfect synchronicity the door burst open. Peter got out of the car and two heavyset men helped him to extract Jack's unconscious neighbour and bundle him through the door, which slammed shut. Peter returned to the car and waited for instructions.

"Liverpool," Amanda said, and he turned the car and moved off at a sedate pace. This abduction had taken no more than ten minutes, which was frightening on many levels. Jack had questions, but they could wait. It was clear that Groucho had been the only active unit which had achieved its objective as, in rapid succession, first Gummo, then Chico and Harpo reported their failure. "Keep looking and report," she told them.

Sitting in the rear seats alongside Jack, she said, "You'll want to know what that was all about?"

Talk about asking the blindingly obvious. "If you please."

"Quite a neat job," she said, stretching her legs out in front of her.

"What about the other cars?"

Amanda laughed a little. "Well, our other cars were trying to pick up our three little pigs, the closest associates of our car salesman. By the way, we think he might have been related to Samms."

"And you missed all three?"

"Yes, and the funny thing is that this was our second go. And" – she lowered her voice even though there was no one else in the car but the three of them – "our enquiries would suggest that they are missing – not at work and no one has seen them."

"Perhaps they were all in it together and have cleared off."

"No, I think she's got them."

"Who? Samms?" He had an image of Samms mercilessly administering rough justice and shivered. "Maybe, but who was our guest?"

She laughed a little. "Oh, that was Colonel Mike Shaw – up-and-coming member of Army Intelligence and, of course, the Whitehall boss of Colonel Braid."

"You mean he's a colleague?" This hadn't been what he'd expected at all.

At this, even Amanda's subordinate allowed himself a laugh and Amanda said, "Well, of a sort. We are on the same side, but our agencies are structured and organised a little differently so that no individual agency achieves excessive influence. It's a safeguard of sorts. However, it can result in some conflicts in short-term objectives."

"So it seems," Jack said wryly.

She ignored this. "Colonel Shaw cannot be trusted at this point. He's probably okay, but we can hardly risk it."

"But is there no other way?"

"I can't think of one, and this will keep him out of the game until we've finished. Then we should have a clearer idea of any possible involvement. He'll be fine – we're just looking after him for a few days."

Jack lit a cigarette and slumped down in the seat. It was more than eight hours until they would set out over rough seas for the Isles of Grace, and already he felt exhausted and very old.

Chapter 35

Cora Samms took a long drag of her cheroot and looked across the ocean from her front lawn.

She would miss the place, but it was a very small sacrifice. Whatever else it had been for the last thirty-five years, it wasn't home. Not for her, and not for the many displaced people she represented.

Home was far away geographically, but never far away from her heart. Today it felt nearer. Her plans wouldn't take her and her people all the way, but they would change the game. The scheme had been long in the planning and, as with any plan, serendipity had played its part.

In the late seventies, facing flight, she could have chosen anywhere. The Isles had been an improbable choice. The Falklands War broke out and created the unlikely requirements of the British Government for a research facility so secret that only these isles could serve. Even then, there had been work to do and it hadn't been simple. Months of private diplomacy, subtle assessments of the effectiveness and durability of potential agents, all over-arched with a critical decision on timing.

She had one shot, and if she missed, it might be generations before another opportunity arose. But there was nothing she had overlooked – she was sure of it.

James Fay approached, coming up from the harbour where he

had been checking and re-checking the vessel. His features were, customarily, impassive and his manner as formal as ever. "I think we are ready, ma'am."

"Thank you, James. Now we must think – what could go wrong? What have we overlooked? Is there more we can do?"

Fay considered for a moment. "Colonel Braid is very nervous now, like a cat on hot bricks. But he can do nothing. He's isolated, has no means of communicating and has no idea who to trust."

"This is unfortunate. I had hoped that we could avoid alerting our neighbours."

"I'm afraid it is too late for that, ma'am."

"Are we absolutely sure Colonel Braid has no means of communicating with the mainland?"

"Yes, his radio's totally out of order – it cannot be restored without a replacement part and that is at least two days off. There are no other deliveries scheduled. His satellite phones are also out of action."

"And you sure we have control on Lessor?"

Fay spoke confidently. "Our man is ready to do what is necessary."

Samms looked out to the ocean again. "And our rendezvous?"

"On time. Not more than a day's sailing away."

"The materials are safe?"

"Yes, I have them quite safe. They travel with me. We aim to be alongside our ship in half an hour. The transfer, a few minutes only."

"Can we be intercepted?"

He shifted on his feet slightly. "There's a theoretical chance of interception, ma'am, but we would have to be very unlucky. There's a one in a thousand chance a Royal Navy destroyer will be within range at the time of transfer."

She nodded. "So, this time the odds are on our side. Besides, their proximity may not matter. We shall see."

Fay had nothing else to report, and on any other day, she would have dismissed him promptly. But this was not any day. She resumed her scan across the ocean. He stood passive at her side. "Are we are doing the right thing, James?" she asked eventually

His reply was instant and resolute. "Yes, ma'am."

"Many will condemn us."

"Only our enemies, ma'am."

"Is there anything you wish to say, James?"

His features did not soften, nor did his strong voice waver. "It has been a privilege to serve you and our people."

She turned and looked at him for a second –perhaps for the last time. She nodded and he bowed in return.

"Now, about our immediate family – how is Angela getting on? We must avenge the death of Ardishar, but we must do justice."

Chapter 36

Angela Delap was working when Fay arrived and she did not look up at his entrance. He poured himself a strong coffee and sat down beside her. "Any progress?"

"A bit. I'm confident that all of them believe that only they are captive. The music has kept them awake for about twenty hours, and of course kills any sound from the other cells. I've told them all that I know they killed Ash and that they've got another eight hours to confess. If they don't, well, they know they will die."

"And are any of them talking?"

"No, not yet, but" – she gestured to the screens in front of her – "they are cracking."

Fay had a look for himself. The images were superficially similar: a single occupant in a small, barely furnished cell.

Jimmy Trent sat motionless and bare-chested in a corner of his cell. Once or twice he looked up and stared straight into the camera. "He's a tough one," Fay said. "He put up a hell of a fight when we picked him up. Put three good men down. Be careful with him. If he remembers his special forces training, it'll take a lot more than a day to break him."

Angela smiled. "Maybe, but the others are not so tough."

Fay's gaze moved to the next monitor, which showcased the agitated form of Dr Laura Gibson. She paced back and forward with frenetic speed, often crashing into the concrete walls.

Sometimes she followed up by crashing her knuckles against the wall with feeble, frantic punches. He turned up audio reception from the cell. She was talking to herself with occasional bursts of tuneless singing and then loud sobs and random screams.

"She's ready to go," Fay said.

"Maybe, another hour or so."

The occupant of the third cell was even more satisfactory.

Jasper Hunt's already embattled constitution had pretty much collapsed, and he lay prone on the floor with only occasional whimpers audible. His hands were pressed tightly over his ears.

Fay turned up the music. "This one's ready."

"You sure?" Angela asked.

Fay was. "We are running out of time. The police file is clear."

"Who do you fancy?"

He shrugged. "Well, the soldier was pissed about money and he knows how to kill."

Angela nodded.

"As for the girl, she met Ash a lot of times recently. Maybe just a girlfriend. The police file has her as a person of significant interest, but I wasn't able to find out why."

His voice hardened when he studied the third monitor. "The doctor, he's just a scumbag. Made a bit on the side with drugs. Ash mentioned him to me a few months ago. I was going to start investigating him, but I never got round to it. Ash had something on him, I think." Back to practicalities. "Anyway, we haven't got twelve hours. There are still a lot of things to do. Give it two more hours, maximum."

"Have you got anything else from the mainland?" Angela asked.

"Nothing. We have to finish this ourselves."

"And if they don't break?"

Fay looked at her hard. There was no time, and they might all be dead tomorrow. As the heir to the long-vacated throne of the Sassanid Empire, the victim was no ordinary one. This death could not be unavenged, and it would be, whatever it took.

"Kill them all."

Chapter 37

At about four, Jack was roughly woken for the second time that day. Again, the guilty party was Amanda Barratt. She looked fresh and alert. He felt like shit. In response to her promptings, he tumbled off the cheap single bed and onto a carpet which could just about qualify as tired.

He groaned in response to the impact from the fall on his tired old bones. The carpet smelled bad – and so did he. Tired as he was, his current position was inimical to further sleep so, with no realistic alternatives, he screwed up his face, tensed his limbs and prepared to stand up. It wasn't easy but he managed it, at least for a moment or two, before giving up again and sitting, head bowed, on the bed end.

Amanda was ignoring him, perusing the ancient maps which Baxter had supplied. He rose, lit a cigarette and, with an effort, made his way over to her. There was only one chair and she gave no sign that she would yield it to her elder, so he went back to the end of the bed.

Without turning, she threw a buff folder which landed at his feet. "Here, have a look at this."

In the absence of anything better to do he reached down with a groan, picked it up and began to peruse the two A4 sheets inside.

It consisted of about twenty names in all, three of whom he already knew from his dinner engagement of the previous evening.

The other seventeen, a mixture of scientists, technicians and a few ancillary staff, could well be involved in any potential conspiracy, but there was nothing by way of a clue. "Is this everyone?"

"Yes, that's the full staff, but the good news is that this posting comes with some perks, and the staff, except the three commanding officers, enjoy generous leave provisions. Including a twelve-week break in the summer."

"So, how many are going to be there when or if we get there?"

"When," Amanda said firmly. "Right now, the facility has a complement of six in total – the three officers, a single scientist and two ancillary staff."

Jack considered this information. "Well, that sounds a bit easier."

"Yes, I think so."

"And it seems improbable that a potential conspirator would be absent at this potentially critical time, so that narrows the field."

"Maybe."

He was on a roll. "Do you think the officers are involved?"

"Must be."

"All of them?"

Amanda shrugged. "I don't know enough about the command and the work processes, but it's got to be at least one. You've met them – who is it?"

"Surely Braid's out?"

She considered. "Well, he could be covering his tracks."

Jack shook his head. "If he is, he's a great actor. No, Braid was terrified."

"And the other two?"

Jack thought back to them all sitting around Cora Samms' table. "They looked as if they hated each other, but who knows? Johnston's a pain in the arse, and Harris has just given up. You must have records on these guys."

"Yes, both exemplary. Harris and Johnston are really good scientists, alpha-plus students, PHDs, the lot."

"Well, either this posting doesn't suit them or they've lost their edge. They looked all in to me."

He threw the papers on the ground and, feeling some strength returning, risked getting to his feet and made his way over to Amanda. "You got a route?"

"Well, if this map is right, and that's a big if, the steep cliffs break in the middle with a low, gradually ascending gap maybe fifty yards wide." She pointed. "It gets a bit steeper after that, but it's no more than a scramble of a couple of hundred feet. From there we're at pretty much the high point of Lessor and then it's downhill, about half a mile, to the base."

It sounded quite easy, and with only six on the island, he was feeling a bit better about the venture. Then he looked out of the window and across at a number of berthed boats bobbing up and down on a moderate swell. He felt sick again.

Chapter 38

Jack and Amanda spent a couple of hours smoking before she got up with a purpose in mind. "You need to have a look at these guns." She threw a handgun beside him on the bed. The magazine followed.

"You ready?"

"I suppose so."

"Eyes shut and no cheating."

Amanda insisted he practise loading and reloading the gun. "This one's a bit different from the Glock."

Maybe, but he didn't remember much about Glock either.

"This is a single-action gun, meaning it needs to be cocked before firing. Okay?"

He nodded.

"If things get warm, keep it cocked but with the safety on. This one has a safety."

He'd like to think these were unnecessary precautions, but he wasn't convinced. He hated using guns, but it was worse when others used guns on him. He spent a little more time getting used to the weight and balance of the firearm until he felt comfortable with it.

After handgun practice, Amanda again dipped into the holdall and produced a modern-looking gun which turned out to be a Borelli M4, a semi-automatic shotgun. Apparently, it was 12 gauge, smooth-bored and the Rolls Royce of shotguns. She explained a lot of details, but it was complicated. It was enough he knew how to load and how to fire it. A decent shot would blow a man's head off at about fifty yards.

In response to Amanda's observations on the grenades, Jack lit up a cigarette. He was sick of his "basic training". Amanda was usually a stickler for detail, but maybe judging that he should not be pushed too far too early, said, "That's enough for now. But I haven't even covered the weapons that they hold on the facility."

It was an unwelcome reminder that folk sometimes fired back.

A knock at the door interrupted them and, with caution and her fingers on her gun, Amanda answered to admit Peter, bearing takeaway food and some news.

"The inflatable is on the supply vessel now and everything else is ready. Your cover story is that you are environmental scientists and have chartered a lift. As to the captain, Davis is his name. He owes Baxter, and he knows what to do. I've confirmed the timings and co-ordinates, and everything looks okay. The crew have loaded up and they re-join the boat at six. You get on at five thirty and Davis will stow you in a private berth. You stay there throughout. He will launch an inflatable for the last leg."

"Have you ever used one of those?" Jack asked Amanda.

"Well, once or twice."

It was once or twice more than he had.

It was nearly five now, and they had barely enough time to eat some soggy burgers before leaving their temporary billet. A short walk led to a modern harbour which was home to a large supply vessel about a couple of hundred feet long, used to supply oil rigs and other marine facilities with a range of necessities. It seemed a reasonable cover, and at least the boat had a legitimate excuse for being somewhere in the North Atlantic.

The main deck area was home to bundles of pipework, various fabrications and dozens of storage containers. They wove their way across the crude metal flooring, and, after a longish walk, they arrived at a two-storey forward area. Peter led them up exposed metal steps and they entered a very modern bridge area stuffed with monitors, controls, and bewildering electronic equipment. A couple of sumptuous luxury chairs either side of a central plinth granted extensive panoramic views. Seated upon one of those was a heavyset man of about fifty poring over a newspaper. He made no attempt either to rise or greet them.

They waited for a moment, but as the man seemed engrossed in the paper, Amanda moved round the plinth and stood in front of him. This partially did the trick and he slowly laid down the paper.

"Miss Barratt?"

She nodded in acknowledgement.

"We're set to leave at seven and, with a decent run, I'll drop you off about eight tomorrow night." Captain Davis followed up with the right answer to her next unspoken question. "Aye, there'll be enough light for you at that time."

He added a word of caution. "We've got 280 nautical miles to go, and I'll have to average about twelve knots, which is a fair lick." He rose at this point. "This way."

They followed him, and a short walk took them to a moderately sized office-like room which was home to a couple of bunks. "We call this the captain's cabin. You'll be comfortable here." He indicated a small, spartan en-suite bathroom and a tiny kitchen, which contained a kettle and a surprisingly well-stocked fridge with a decent selection of ready meals and other foodstuffs.

Amanda nodded and Davis finished his tour by telling them that on no account should they leave the room. He indicated a nondescript button on the wall. "If you need to speak to me, just press here." Pleasant as he was, his expression made it clear there were almost no circumstances that could make a summons necessary. "Okay?"

Amanda nodded and Peter dropped the canvas holdalls on to a side table, and, after Amanda had a quick chat with him, he and Davis left.

There was nothing else to do but wait for the thick end of the day. Jack drifted to the lower bunk and lay back while Amanda, in a moderately touching domestic scene, brought him a cup of strong, black coffee, squeezed his arm, then sat down on an occasional chair without another word.

Chapter 39

Two hundred and eighty nautical miles away, Angela Delap, despite her new deadline, had been making glacial progress with her investigations. Then a further stolen police report appeared in her email account, and although it contained little information, it was at least new information. In short, it placed Jasper Hunt near, very near, to the area where Ash had been murdered. It wasn't that much, but it supported the prevailing direction of her enquiry. She glanced at the individual monitors. The condition of both Trent and Gibson was pretty much as before, but Hunt was fading fast.

Delap had sought to accelerate this process by leaving a bottle of whisky in the cell. Hunt was a doctor. He knew it wouldn't help. He finished the bottle. The alcohol had significantly accelerated the degradation of his facilities, and in addition to his pitiful physical state, he was now talking to himself incessantly. No one with a heart could have failed to be moved. No one could refuse sympathy to a human being reduced to this.

How she could afflict him further? She rose slowly and made her way down the short flight of stairs. A moment later she entered the windowless, claustrophobic cell in which Hunt was losing touch with the world of men. He was lying face down on the floor, so she shouted a request and a moment later her brother appeared and, at her bidding, lifted Hunt with ease and placed him on a chair.

To maintain Hunt's position required her brother to stand

alongside, and he did so as she conducted a simple interrogation. "Did you give Ash drugs?"

Hunt peered through his one open eye. "Can I have another drink?"

Angela indicated to her brother, who left and then returned with another bottle of the poisonous spirit. She handed the bottle to Hunt and he seemed temporarily revived. Another slug of the whisky perked him up further and, for a moment, he looked almost happy.

And then he made a decision Angela knew he would regret: he started talking. She asked him again, gently this time, "Did you supply him with drugs?"

"Yes, a few times, but I'm a doctor, not a drug dealer."

She nodded pleasantly enough, encouraging him to continue.

"He forced me to supply him, you see."

Angela did not see, but she knew that things would become clear enough soon.

Hunt took another slug of the whisky and cast a leery smile at her. She responded in kind and, in slurred tones, he continued almost wistfully. "He made me do it, you see. Blackmail, it was."

Angela no longer needed to prompt, just to wait.

"He recognised me from years back. From Tunisia. We were trialling a new drug and we needed a few students to try them out. The trials were quite successful, mostly." He shrugged. "Well, mistakes sometimes happen. A few side effects and a couple of deaths – think one of them was a friend of Ash's."

Some of our people. Her pulse was racing now, but she needed to remain calm. The whole story would soon emerge.

Hunt protested his bona fides further. "I told Ash no more drugs, no more, but he kept going on about it. I told him 'No, I'm a doctor' – I wanted to help him."

It was useless as a plea of mitigation, but Hunt nodded to himself. He had another slug of whisky.

"Well, he was going to expose me – said he'd go to the BMA,

to the papers. I'd have been ruined."

He should have opted for an audience with the BMA rather than where he was now, Angela thought.

"Tried to blackmail me, took me for thousands of pounds." He screwed up his eyes, emitted a low moan, and moved a little towards her. He whispered, "And there is nothing worse than a blackmailer, nothing."

Delap did not agree with this assertion, but she did not say so. There were many things worse than a blackmailer and they included a corrupt, dissolute doctor who had killed a Persian prince.

Angela's brother yanked back his supporting arm and Hunt crashed forward and lay face down before her. The fall did not shut him up, however, and his discourse continued; this time, a blend of high-pitched, continual and hollow laughter.

It was too much for Angela Delap. Professional detachment deserted her. "Stop it, stop!"

In response, the laughter became more insistent and more urgent, and through the hysteria he repeated, "Nothing worse than a blackmailer."

Angela knelt down beside him. She had seen and heard enough. She grasped his greasy, greying hair and pulled so hard that his head jerked up violently. He looked straight at her and she moved her own face a little nearer. His was a broken face. He tried a smile.

She drew her pistol, shoved it hard against his face and fired a single round, leaving both the back wall and her elegant suit jacket decorated with technicolour matter from the skull of the late Dr Jasper Hunt.

Chapter 40

It might have been the captain's cabin, but it felt small to Jack and was getting smaller every single, slow minute of the journey. He had always suspected he was claustrophobic, but had not realised how acute it had become. Heightening the displeasurable experience was the fact that they could not leave the room. Although he rationalised that his confinement was illusory – he had only to walk to the door and open it – he could not get his brain to accept this simple truth. The thought of opening the bland door became almost an obsession, and to control his racing heart he was talking to himself inaudibly but incessantly. Mostly these strictures didn't work and, when not focusing upon the door, he found himself reacting increasingly to what, for most, would have been the gentle rolling of the vessel as it laboured through the treacle-like sea to their destination.

Amanda was on the top bunk and probably sleeping. He hoped she was; if not, her silence might imply nervousness on her part. He couldn't handle that. His irrational brain needed something to believe in, and the only thing he could believe in was her calm assurance. If she believed that they might survive this confinement, the journey, and the mission, then it might, just might, turn out all right.

There was an upside to his claustrophobic terrors, and it was that total preoccupation with something so benign as being in an ample-sized room for a few hours was distracting him from making a more accurate risk assessment of his more immediate future. This temporary confinement would end; but only a man who had lost his reason would favour exchanging it for a landing by inflatable onto an island of uncertain topography, followed by a mission which may well get them both killed.

It did occur to him once, and he thought hard about it for a few seconds before returning to his central obsession of leaving this room. He could expunge the thought, but he caught a break at last, for he was also physically exhausted. Although, with a mind revving in the red zone, proper sleep was out of the question, intermittent bouts of unconsciousness intruded from time to time. After one such bout, he perked up a little when he realised that nearly three precious hours had disappeared.

By Jack's reckoning they were now about a third of the way into the journey. He lit a cigarette and cursed. Take it like a man, for Christ's sake. He managed for a little while by philosophising as to why a pleasurable experience which lasted sixteen hours would be over in a flash, whereas the remaining journey time would seem interminable.

A moment later, he was again focusing on the cabin door, elevating its importance minute by minute until it became the gateway to paradise. After satisfactorily managing to waste another three hours of his potentially soon-to-be ended life, Jack's saviour descended in the unlikely mortal cloak of Captain Davis. And he blessed Davis, for he managed something that Jack could not by opening the door and offering them a chance to stretch their legs outside.

Apparently, the crew were between twelve-hour shifts and custom and practice dictated that a perfect handover was never achieved. With faltering steps, Jack followed Davis back to the bridge, and relief turned to elation when Davis indicated a small wicket door which opened easily and led to a narrow-fenced balcony. Jack leant carelessly on the low railings and, in between deep drags of a cigarette, gulped huge lungfuls of the clean air.

As he had hoped, and despite his fears, the wind was light and the weather clement. The ocean or sea was accordingly calm and from this vantage point he could detect almost no roll from the ship. Progress seemed to be sure and the ship powered through the water, leaving huge, brilliant white wakes on either side. No land was visible; he imagined that they were clear of the Ulster coast and were in the Atlantic Ocean. He hoped this meant that they were ahead of schedule, but his hopes were dashed a moment later as Amanda joined him. "We're about half an hour behind – something to do with wind and currents."

Standing outside with the wind through his hair, he could just about handle this news. She mirrored his position, leaning over the rail of the balcony. Under other circumstances, this would have been an idyllic and sensational experience. The views and prospects from this forward position were thrilling, and the girl by his side the stuff of dreams.

She was very near to him and became even nearer as she nestled into him. She smelled good as well, despite the long drive, the cheap hotel and the confinement of the cabin. Her thick black hair danced across the side of his face, and, for an all too brief moment, Jack was happy, worrying neither about the past nor the future. The present was all that mattered, and he shut his eyes, gently enjoying the moment.

Unfortunately, a moment was all he was granted. Davis stuck his head through the wicket door and announced that they must return to their cell. They both complied, but Amanda seemed reluctant too. This time the return to the cabin was made at least more bearable by the sight of a good deal of food laid on a table. Surprisingly, the fare was not what Jack had imagined; not for Davis or his crew bacon butties and stewed tea. A crew, just like an army, apparently ran on its stomach, and Jack chewed on a few asparagus tips before sampling some salmon, then settling on a plateful of lean fillet steak with a glass of far-from-ordinary red plonk.

The food revived both their spirits and, when they were replete, it was obvious that sleep would come. After a last mouthful of the passable burgundy, Jack headed over to the lower bunk. This time he was ready for sleep.

Chapter 41

In her subterranean art gallery on the Island of Main, Cora Samms was pacing around her collection, from time to time looking down at a sheaf of papers. Occasionally she would make a short annotation or instruction, but mostly she was enjoying the collection for the last time in a while. Despite the thoroughness of the arrangements, it might be the last time ever. She expelled the idea quickly, but it encouraged her to make the most of this brief window.

Unfortunately, the window proved a little shorter than she had hoped as first James Fay and then Angela Delap invaded her shrine. They stood together and a little way away. Cora broke off from a last appreciation of a Cézanne still life and nodded, whereupon they both approached her.

"We have finished," Fay said. "We have identified and dealt with the murderer of Mr Ashanti."

Cora didn't ask for further details. "Thank you."

"What about the others?"

"Are they innocent?"

"Yes, we think so."

"If they are innocent, they should be released," she said. "Can we arrange that?"

"Yes, we can time-lock the cells."

"Very well. Do this and they can take their chances. Now what of our plans?"

"The ship will be ready by ten o'clock," Fay said. "There are no reports of any difficulties and the nearest British ship is currently twelve hours sailing away, following a benign course as far as we are concerned."

"Good. We must finish crating the pictures."

Angela Delap, in a fresh, untainted business suit, nodded and said, "I will send the men up now."

Fay turned to leave also, but Samms held him back. "James, a word."

"Yes, ma'am."

"There are a few things I should like to discuss with you. I had hoped we would have a little more time to make our departure arrangements, but it now seems prudent to bring these arrangements forward. We cannot be sure the Colonel has not shared his concerns, and who knows how the British might react." She sighed. "I like the British, but I'm not sure I understand them. All pragmatism and no passion. Nevertheless, they have endured."

"Yes, ma'am," Fay contributed, and then asked, "Can we trust the British?"

Samms considered. "We can only trust them to pursue their own interests. However, in this case our interests are, at least, partially aligned. They also would prefer Persia to Islamic Iran." She cut to practicalities. "So, James. Two devices to the Israelis and retain two."

"Yes, ma'am, but you will oversee it, of course."

She hesitated.

"Ma'am?"

"We are in challenging times, James. Who is to say? Remember, the Sasanian people will never give up the struggle. Remember Neharend in 642AD. We have dreamt of this since then."

And now the dream was almost a reality.

Chapter 42

Jack awoke to rough shaking. This time, rather than welcoming the wake-up call, he was consumed by sleep, and he turned away from Amanda, avoiding the moment of truth for as long as possible. She banged around the cabin, making coffee and emptying and re-packing and checking the contents of the canvas bags. Part of him still wanted to sleep, but when he heard the unmistakeable sound of an unloaded Browning pistol being cocked and clicked, he knew it was time to get up.

He felt terrible and tried without success to fashion his hair into something acceptable in public. She seemed to be indifferent to his appearance and continued playing with the Brownings until satisfied they were fit for whatever their purpose proved to be. She threw him a cigarette and looked at him. "You all right?"

He nodded untruthfully, lit the cigarette and stretched wearily.

"Okay, we need to get these suits on." She got up and turned away from him, and a moment later stood completely naked, battling with her dry suit. It was tough not to look. He looked. He needed to know how to put the thing on, and besides, maybe it would be the last time.

It was no time for modesty so he joined in and threw his clothes aside and then spent a frustrating few minutes until the suit was eventually on. It was inconveniently heavy. He hoped the landing would be straightforward. Somehow, he doubted it, but he busied himself by checking clothes and provisions in the two canvas holdalls. They were precious, and he was detailed to guard them through the trip.

He located two heavy plastic sheets and fashioned them into outer protectors for the bags, while Amanda occupied herself with a final, last-minute perusal of the ancient and possibly doubtful maps. They were ready to go.

Davis didn't keep them long. Without a word, they followed him back through the bridge and down two storeys to the main cargo deck. The area was empty of crew. They were led past the containers and pipework to the end of the boat. Thankfully, the wind was light and the weather fair. Then he looked over a low rail and noted that the descent from the cargo deck looked to be more than twenty feet, but it varied alarmingly as the ocean swelled and receded around the ship.

Davis looked out to sea. "Aye, you'll probably make it." With this confident endorsement, he took a step backwards and said to Jack, "Right, take an end."

A small inflatable craft had been readied for the next steps. At either end, a thick wet rope was attached.

It wasn't very heavy, which was concerning, and it was very easy for Davis and Jack to lower it to the sea. It was a lot more difficult to keep it steady and adjacent to the ship. Davis tied his rope to the rail and then roped Amanda. It was only about twenty rungs, but it took the athletic Amanda a little time to get to the bottom. She roped herself to the bottom rung and Davis again held the inflatable. It moved three dimensionally, never still, and Amanda took her time before choosing her moment. Then she was in, and after tying and untying ropes she secured the inflatable to the bottom rung of the metal ladder.

Next the bags and their plastic veneers were individually and carefully lowered. Amanda placed them in a space within the casing that supported a central steering wheel.

Then it was Jack's turn. Davis roped him and he threw a leg

over the side. His trip was theoretically a little easier. As he descended, the powerful outboard motor burst into life. Amanda was more accomplished than she had modestly advised. With the rope anchoring the craft and selective use of the power, she was able to stabilise the craft.

The ladder rungs were wet and thin and were set too near to the ship's hull, allowing space for about a third of his foot. He had a single minor slip and, at the last rung, a short alarming moment with the snapping ocean below him before she manoeuvred the boat underneath.

Amanda held his legs and he released one hand and then, with his eyes shut, another. He fell, but she grabbed him and he achieved a safe, if inelegant, embarkation. There was only one seat, and that was for the pilot.

She indicated a space beside her. "Sit down, keep low, don't move and hold onto this ring." She completed what looked like some final checks, flashed a signal at Davis, who returned the gesture, and they were off.

Jack gripped firmly onto the rude handle and made himself comfortable. When he looked round, the supply ship seemed a long way back, and they were on their own.

Ahead, the cliffs of the Isles of Grace rose up from the ocean. They looked reassuringly near. He pointed them out enthusiastically, but estimation of distance at sea was very difficult and his heart sank as Amanda shouted, "Sorry, half an hour."

For the first five minutes, the journey was more exhilarating than nauseating, but he rapidly tired of the constantly changing view as the craft thumped into swell after swell. Things went from bad to worse when a huge wall of water crashed into his face and he involuntarily swallowed what seemed like pints of foul, salty ocean.

A second later he felt sick, and a second after that he was sick. He hung over the side, retching violently. The retching passed, allowing the fear to take over. He raised his head slowly and, as he did so, he felt the inflatable slow a little. When he looked up, the reason why became clear. The island was close. Maybe they were early? Then he realised what had led to her time estimate. The final stretch was going to be more challenging than the tumultuous ride across the open ocean.

The swell was reduced now, but the difficulty was charting a path through gaps between razor-sharp basalt outcrops. The night was still fine and there was a good hour of daylight left, but this time was quickly used up as Amanda made numerous fruitless sweeps before determining the final route.

This route was not immediately obvious to Jack, but as she moved the inflatable alongside the lethal black rocks, he saw that she was right and there was a narrow passage. It would have been wider when the antiques map had been charted, but what must have been a huge rockfall now made the going challenging.

Amanda's seamanship was impressive, and she charted a way around the last of the sharp black rocks. With the rocks now behind them, they now proved helpful as a partial shield from the open ocean. She delicately wedged the inflatable between two more rounded rocks and brought the craft to a gentle halt in a small sheltered lagoon. "Get ready, we can get off here," she said.

They each took a bag and he followed her through a hundred yards of waist-high water. It was calm, but the flow was still powerful and not always in their favour. It was strength-sapping work before they made land at the base of a cliff. The land began with a narrow strip of flat sandy ground, which was as close to a beach as they were going to get. They both flung themselves down. Jack's lungs were bursting and Amanda allowed him a few minutes.

"Right, that's long enough. Get changed."

They removed the dry suits and changed into heavy boots and a selection of rough, khaki clothes. They weren't the greatest fit, but after the dry suit, Jack would have taken anything.

A tedious and difficult scramble lay ahead, made more difficult when carrying heavy holdalls, but this was achieved at the cost of only a few knocks. When the cliff was overcome it was now close to ten, and, as Davis had forecast, there was more than enough light to show that they were now on solid ground – and the highest point of the island. Again, they sat: she to review the general situation and next steps, and he because he was exhausted.

After a moment or two recovering, he half sat up. It was a good vantage point.

"You okay?" Amanda asked. Without waiting for an answer, she continued. "Now there …" She indicated the outline of several low buildings, one of which had a light burning. "That's the buildings of our facility. There is currently a skeleton staffing – Braid, the other two officers and three others. At this time of night everything should be pretty quiet – so the plan is that we get down there and hopefully catch up with Braid in his quarters. After that, we'll play it as we see it."

Play it as she saw it. He had faith in her command, though – certainly more than in his.

Command allowed him a cigarette, but did not extend the break. She insisted that he slip on a holster and load a Browning, which he did. With that, they set off for half a mile or so on a pleasant, downhill stretch, stumbling occasionally in response to the hard, irregular ground and thick, wild grasses. The night was still fine and reasonably warm, and in other circumstances the walk would have been pleasant.

But where they were going cast a pall over the whole journey.

Chapter 43

Colonel John Braid sat alone in his quarters. They consisted of three rooms: a bedroom, a small sitting room and a large office, from which most of his administrative business was conducted. It was also home to the broken-down radio which had so catastrophically failed, rendering him deaf and blind at this most desperate of times. Luck had not completely deserted him, however, and a replacement radio had been ordered some weeks ago, even before the current inconvenience. It would be here in forty-eight hours via the monthly supply ship which served the islands. Would that be soon enough?

Over the last forty-eight hours, what had begun as vague suspicions had become certainties, and a problem which might have been an accounting error had instead been confirmed as very deliberate theft. Things were stolen every day, all over the world, he reasoned as he poured himself another large brandy, but this theft was a little different. Losing a single miniature nuclear smart bomb would certainly not be dismissed as an accident, and to lose four, he was sure, would be thought worse than careless.

His career was certainly over – even if the items were recovered – but Braid had never really much cared for his career. Even although he had little else in his life – no wife, no children, no special interests – he had always been, inexplicably, happy. He had no idea why, but it seemed wrong to overanalyse it.

What he did know was that he was unhappy now. He was also scared, but he was also finding out something else about himself in these desperate and changed circumstances. He had courage, and he determined that he would use this unexpected discovery in leading and correcting the current emergency.

All day he had been engaged mostly in desk research, seeking to gain a mental picture of what exactly was going on under his command, and now he was very much clearer. Individual parts for the technologically advanced devices were not as rigorously stock-controlled as the enriched plutonium which fuelled them, but there was still an accounting process of sorts. Detailed review of pages of documents, plus a physical count, confirmed that no fewer than two and probably not more than four complete devices could be assembled from the stolen component parts. Once that had been achieved, the riskier task of providing their fuel would begin.

Given the likelihood that this shortfall must eventually be discovered, it was obvious that the conspiracy was now very well advanced. From his audit today of the plutonium, conducted in secret and without the knowledge of his two subordinates, Braid knew that he must get assistance urgently, but this was easier said than done, not only due to the broken radio but also because of two other – inconvenient – truths.

The first was that even after his investigations, there was no possibility he could trust either of his direct reports. The simple safeguard inherent in the stock-control process made it impossible that a third party could perpetrate the larceny without the knowledge of one or the other. His brain was working well now. Both could not be in alliance. If that was so, it was unlikely the discrepancy would have shown up in the stocktake reports. They would have simply contrived to falsify the records, so it was probable that only one of them was a traitor.

Unfortunately, he had not yet worked out which, and he was not all that sure how to go about the investigation. At a dead end, he turned his mind back to his second key problem.

Either Cora Samms, or at least some of her people, must be involved somehow. The theft was about more than degrading his command, and if someone had gone to the trouble of stealing the devices, they would surely need a means to transport them off the island.

Only Samms and the British armed forces could visit this island, and as the British already owned the physical and intellectual rights to the devices, it seemed improbable that they would seek to steal their own goods. That left Samms and her staff as the only ones capable of moving goods anywhere. No other explanation seemed possible. But how far did this treachery go?

In any event, he could not seek support from those on the sister island. He was completely alone, with no real options but to wait until he could again communicate his plight with the mainland.

However, that was not strictly true; if it was such common knowledge that the radio would soon be restored, the end-game must be near. As far as he could see, he had two chances. If one of his officers was a traitor and one was not, then he had at least one potential ally, and there were also three other staff at the facility who, maybe, he could trust. The challenge, of course, was to identify the traitor. Again, he put this problem on hold and turned to his second chance.

Unbeknownst to anyone else on the island, the radio which had so obviously now been subtly sabotaged was not the original radio which had been posted to the facility. The original radio had accompanied Braid himself in the first days but had almost immediately broken down. This had been before any of the current staff had been in post. An immediate replacement had been shipped but, carelessly, the old one had never been taken away for repair. And so it had sat for years, gathering dust inside an administrative cabinet.

It was an identical model to the current distressed version, and Braid was exploring it now. He was no radio technician, but perhaps some unknown combination of parts might allow him to create a single serviceable model, so he studied the machines carefully for a while.

It had been a great idea, but the task was beyond him. He let his mind drift on to his two subordinates.

Braid did not care for either of them. Superficially, Harris was the worse of the two. He had been in post for about three years. Braid had no idea why Harris was in the army. He hated authority, hated the system, hated, it seemed, everyone and everything. Braid also suspected Harris to be a secret anti-nuclear man, sympathetic to the CND, so why he was applying his considerable brainpower to the cause of creating newer, better and more efficient nuclear weapons, Braid was at a loss to understand.

Still, was it possible that the likes of Harris could be playing some sort of game from the inside which might sabotage the research? Maybe, but he shook his head in perplexity. Harris believed in nothing at all, it seemed, and, in Braid's experience, fanatics always believed in something.

He turned to Johnston, and at first sight everything about Johnston seemed in order. He was a model soldier, believed in queen and country and was an enthusiast for all things military. That was all on the plus side, but Johnston believed in things, unlike the apostate Harris.

Braid had no proof at all, but with each succeeding brandy, his distorted brain, reviewing over and over the same observations, was forcing him to a provisional conclusion. Which one? One or the other, or even both? More than once, his judgement alighted upon one of the soldiers only to transfer, a moment later, to the other until the intense swapping halted, and Braid's brain ceased processing and settled firmly on one of the men.

He knew who the traitor was now, and he would prove it. He also knew which of them he could trust, and he would summon him now and together they would form a plan.

A thought came upon him, and he effected a simple substitution of the fuse of the microphone of the ancient radio to its newer sibling. His heart leapt as the radio sprang into life.

And at that moment, his fortunes improved even further when his junior officer, the one he knew he could trust, appeared in his office doorway.

But as his eyes took in what was in front of him, he knew he was facing the fact he had made a mistake for the last time in his life.

Three rapid rounds from an expertly aimed handgun resigned his commission for ever.

Chapter 44

Jack and Amanda neared the first of the army buildings. The evening was noiseless. Unless, of course, you counted the pistol shots, followed a few minutes later by long bursts of automatic gunfire. Amanda put her hand out and stopped Jack in his tracks. "Leave the bags here." She pointed to a prominent and solitary rock. "You got your gun?"

"Yes."

"Follow me."

The ground was similar to that already traversed, devoid of major obstacles and consisting mostly of long grasses largely blown and broken by prevailing winds.

"Don't leave my side," she said, and broke into a moderate jog.

Adrenalin, and not fitness, allowed him to keep up with her until she pulled up about ten yards from the entrance to Braid's headquarters. Jack was blowing very hard now, and his heart was thumping.

There was no window in the gable end of the Portakabin, but some light was streaming from another window at the front.

With difficulty, he brought his breathing under control while Amanda frantically looked left and right. There were two choices. Front or back. She chose the back of the cabin and, this time in very deliberate paces, led them forward until they stood against the construction. There was a window at the back of the building and

Amanda thrust her head forward slowly. Jack did also, but an effective blind blocked the view from inside.

"No good. Let's go to the front," she said.

They retraced their steps. The front window was blinded also, so they moved past it and onto a narrow, paved walkway. Jack followed Amanda closely, occasionally looking behind as they shuffled along. A few yards on, the structure receded to reveal a clear plastic-looking walkway which connected to a further modular building. It was bisected by a rough door. Dim light from the walkway cast its presence on to the concrete surround and the rough grassland beyond.

They waited and listened. The silence was total. What lay within was a complete mystery, but there was only one way to find out.

Amanda looked at him. She held his arm and put her mouth to his ear. "I'm going to the door. Keep a pace or two behind me."

Her voice just carried over the sound of his thumping heart. He nodded and they moved forward – she to the door and he two paces behind.

Amanda pulled down the door handle, which gave a low, unoiled squeak, barely perceptible but deafening to Jack. Very deliberately, she depressed the handle. She pulled the door towards her, and in slow motion pushed her head forward into the narrow passageway and looked left and right.

A short, sharp burst of automatic fire from the main building made up her mind and she sprang into the walkway. With gun pointing, she turned both ways and then shouted to him. "In!"

Jack followed through the door. She turned and began running back towards the first building. The passageway broadened into a perfectly ordered, sparsely furnished lounge-cum-reception room which was at perfect peace. Off the room were two doors, one closed and the other ajar, and it was from the open door that the light source emanated.

"Stand there. Cover that door," Amanda shouted.

He did so while she crashed through the closed door before

emerging a few seconds later and declaring the room clear. As the other door was ajar, she used this natural advantage to inch through it gun first with infinite slowness and caution.

Gradually, she pushed the door fully open and, with care, checked for hostile activity behind the door, behind the large office desk and even behind a tall set of metal cabinets. He followed her in.

It was a large room kitted out as a standard office. White noise from a radio set in the corner broke the silence. The metal filing cabinets were well-ordered and the desk was tidy. The room was unremarkable in every way. Except for the body of Colonel Braid slumped over his desk with half of his face missing.

Amanda moved to the body, conducted a crude investigation and unnecessarily declared him dead. "Well, that's Braid in the clear. You okay?"

Jack laughed humourlessly, but already felt sick. "Fine. What now?"

"There are six people in this facility. One at least is dead. Let's see about the others."

She led him out of Braid's office and past the connecting walkway. The other side of the walkway began with a large, square lounging area with numerous cheap chairs and tables, a pool table and an ancient radio. The smell of stale cigarettes tickled Jack's nostrils.

Counting had always been one of his few accomplishments, and his razor-sharp brain instantly incremented the number of dead from one to two. No further information was required to conclude that the white-coated individual lying face down in the middle of the room was dead. From at least ten yards away, Jack counted at least six entry or exit wounds, which presumably accounted for at least one of the bursts of automatic fire.

Amanda was a pace or two ahead of him at this point, but she stopped and edged back alongside him. "We need the shotguns."

"Will I go back and get them?"

She considered and said, "I think that would be best. I'll go back to Braid's office and wait. Hurry, and be careful."

He retraced his steps out the door and left the complex. His eyes were now accustomed to the half-light, and after only a few false steps he located the rock, picked up both of the bags, and turned back to the complex.

But before he could return, an unknown sound behind made him freeze.

Chapter 45

Through the wind, the mysterious sound grew stronger, and he threw the bags down and executed a half turn, now scanning the ground away from the buildings in the vague direction of Main.

At first, he could see nothing, but his eyes adjusted and he caught sight of a figure running. The figure was sprinting from the far end of the complex, but at a shallow angle to it.

He was heading across the rough ground and towards the tarmacked road which connected the islands. This route took him progressively closer to Jack and, although well out of range of the light projecting from the buildings, as he neared it was clear the figure was a powerful, athletic man dressed in standard army fatigues.

He didn't know whether the man was armed but, given all the circumstances, it was sensible to assume that he was. Jack might have been able to shoot him with a lucky shot, but his senses were far from scrambled, and he was in enough control to realise that, despite the man's flight, it was not yet clear whether the man was a friend or foe. So, Jack stood and watched.

Then the circumstances changed.

The runner lost his footing and fell heavily onto the rough ground. Jack took his chance. He sprinted towards the man and leapt on top of him.

A second later, he had total control of the situation with a strong grasp of the man's arm, which he twisted behind his back. He held firm for a further few seconds, considering his next move, but the decision was not to be his. With immense strength, the prone man turned the situation on its head, and now he sat across Jack's shoulders, pinning him down with a vice-like hold.

Jack felt the serrated edge of a combat knife pressed hard against his throat. He could see the man's face clearly now. Captain Harris. Identifying the traitor was insufficient compensation for the knowledge of his impending death, and he struggled in vain for what he imagined would be the last time. Harris, however, hesitated.

When he spoke, his voice was emotional. "You bastard. I saw you at dinner. You're one of Samms' bastards. Bastard! I'll kill all of you, one by one, and then I'm going to kill Samms." He indicated the complex with a nod. "You've killed everyone. Why did you have to do that? What's so fucking important?" It was purely rhetorical. The blade pressed harder against Jack's throat.

Jack shut his eyes. The next sounds were unexpected, but they were welcome. They came clearly through the night. "Armed police." The cocking of a Browning accompanied this introduction, and when Jack opened his eyes, there was a gun pressed hard against Harris's temple. Jack was not yet relaxed, given Harris's emotional state, but he did relax a little when in slow, deliberate moves the knife was removed from his throat. The man stood up slowly and released him.

"Who's this?" Amanda asked Jack.

"Captain Harris. I met him at dinner."

"Okay, Captain Harris, this way, very slowly."

The three then headed back to Braid's door: Jack first, Harris second and Amanda behind.

Amanda directed them to Braid's office and pointed Harris to a seat in the far corner. She pulled a long wax coat from a stand and flung it over Braid's body. Jack placed the canvas bags in another corner and Amanda got to work. Dead individuals made for a far easier enquiry, Jack supposed. They could be eliminated from further enquiries, innocent or otherwise. Either way, they were out of the game.

Taking Harris alive, on the other hand, would cause Amanda a complication. If he was an enemy, they would have to devote resources to minding him, whereas if he was innocent then time was being wasted. Worst of all would be if they could not be sure.

"Captain Harris, I am Amanda Barratt of the Home Office. The man you tried to kill is Jack Edwards. I understand you have met Mr Edwards before. This was at the house of Cora Samms, but Mr Edwards is attached to the Home Office and is working with me."

Harris looked at Jack. "I thought you were McLeod?"

"Not tonight," he said.

Having cleared this up, Amanda continued, "So that's who we are. Now what or who are you, Captain Harris?"

Harris's head was bowed, and he looked indescribably sad. If it was an act, it was very convincing. "I'm Captain Harris, a scientist attached to the British Army. A scientist." He looked towards the covered body of Braid. "What the fuck's all that about?"

"I was rather hoping that you would enlighten me, Captain Harris." Her voice was formal, ice-cold and authoritative, and her hand was still on her gun.

He raised his head, ran his fingers through an untidy shock of hair and started to talk with gathering composure. "If you two are on the island, you know there's something going on. Something going on …" He let slip a desperate laugh at the inadequacy of the phrasing. "We have some highly dangerous and highly desirable secrets on this island – miniature nuclear devices. And I believe that Cora Samms is in league with my colleague." He spat out the name. "Captain Johnston has stolen several of these devices." The anger in his voice subsided and he said, feebly, "Have you any idea what damage one of these can do?"

He knew better than anyone the answer to this question, Jack was aware, and he fell silent.

"How do you know that Captain Johnston is involved?" Amanda asked.

It was a good question and Harris had a good answer. "Who do you think I was fucking chasing? I was in bed and heard shots. I got up and ran through here. O'Connor, the scientist, was dead in the mess, and in here Braid was too.

"I went back to the mess and into the kitchen. Our two orderlies – well, they're fucking dead too. So, that left me and Johnston. And I didn't kill anyone. I still supposed that Johnston might be okay and that we were under attack from outside, but then I ran into him with an automatic in his hand. I took one look at him and turned tail. He tried a few shots, but I got away, although he caught me in the leg."

At this point Harris turned his leg round and stuck out a blood-soaked calf.

Amanda eyed him suspiciously. "How do we know that you didn't kill everyone and were wounded in the process? Why were you fleeing?"

Harris was nothing if not honest, apparently. "I suppose you don't. Anyway, I was unarmed and facing a man with a gun. A man who had killed four people. I ran outside and behind a few rocks. I waited. Then he came out. He looked around for a bit, but he didn't see me. Then he headed off. Off to see his fucking boss, Samms."

Harris looked down at his hands. "Well, I sat there for a while. What could I do? Everyone dead, the bad guys in control, and me wounded without any prospect of rescue. Figured I would probably die anyway, so I thought might as well go out in a blaze of glory. You know the rest. Bloody leg gave out on me."

Amanda was silent for a moment and then turned to Jack. "Right, I'm going to take another look around. Make a better job of guarding him than you did the last time."

Jack sat a safe distance from Harris, who exhibited neither energy nor ambition for escape.

Amanda holstered her handgun and delved into the holdall.

After a quick check, she ran out of the office with a shotgun.

Harris asked for a cigarette and Jack lit one and threw it towards him. Harris retrieved it from the floor and began to suck on it frantically. Jack did the same. Was Amanda safe out there? He willed things to stay silent. After a tense few minutes, she was back.

She looked unfazed. "Okay, Captain Harris, you certainly have four dead here. That much is true."

"It's all fucking true," he mumbled.

"What now?" Jack enquired, but she wasn't finished with Harris. Instead, she moved towards Harris, knelt in front of him and began to examine his wounded leg. She tutted and shook her head. "There might be a bullet still in there."

Slowly, and with care, she dressed and bandaged the wound. "There, that should do temporarily." She turned to Jack. "Assuming, just assuming, that Johnston has gone to Samms, they must be ready to go. This is the final act. Getting rid of the witnesses."

This seemed logically sound. "What about him?" Jack jerked his head at Harris.

"Well, even if he is friendly, he's not very mobile."

"He was mobile enough fifteen minutes ago. He nearly killed me. Besides, what's the use of leaving him here? If he's mobile, he could follow us anyway."

Harris interrupted this private discussion. "Look, I could have killed you, but I didn't. I spoke to you – I thought you were one of Samms' men. If I was with them, why would I say that? Anyway, whatever you decide, remember that I can help you across to Main. I know the ground – I know the outbuildings."

"Well, that's true enough," Amanda said. "Besides which, it is a risk leaving him behind."

It was a risk taking him too.

Amanda nodded to Harris. "Okay, you come with us. Any nonsense and I'll put a bullet in you."

In these circumstances it seemed like a very reasonable

condition; after all, who was going to care about another dead body in this madness?

Chapter 46

They each had another cigarette as Amanda emptied both canvas bags, carefully selected the most important of their respective contents and combined them into a single bag. She ditched the food, kept the ammunition and a single medical kit. Jack was granted custody of two handguns and one of the shotguns. He put one of the handguns in his holster, one in his pocket and walked with the shotgun.

Both Amanda and Jack continued stashing until they had accounted for all the ammunition. She flung Harris the bag.

"Do I get a gun?"

"You do not, Captain Harris. Can you walk?"

He got up from the chair inelegantly and spent a bit of time gingerly putting weight on his bad leg until he declared himself fit.

"Now, Captain Harris, we plan to cross to Main. We consider everyone hostile. Given the circumstances we have encountered here, we shoot to kill on contact. So, give us your assessment of what we face."

Harris raised himself up and became a soldier again. "It's about a mile to get to the big house and the going is easy if we follow the road. The land falls away at first until we reach the gap between the islands, which is bridged. After that the road continues – uphill.

"Before the main house, there are three or maybe four cottage-type buildings, but I don't think they are all purely domestic establishments. Alongside the main house and extending west is the fast jet runway, and there are a couple of hangar buildings a little way along. Beyond the house, downhill steeply again to the jetty and harbour."

Amanda listened attentively, then looked at Jack.

"That's how I remember it."

"Strength, capability?" Amanda asked.

"Heavily armed certainly," Harris said. "As to strength, I think, but cannot be completely sure, we are dealing with five, although if they have a boat in the harbour there may be more. There's Samms herself, then Fay." He paused for a moment. "Fay's experienced and dangerous. He's powerful, capable and I wouldn't be surprised if he's been a soldier."

Jack nodded to Amanda.

"Then there are the two Delaps – brother and sister. He's a large, powerful man and I've never heard him speak. As for her, I think she's a business manager who looks after artworks or something like that. She seems pleasant enough, but who's to say?"

Jack thought back to their silent walk together. Pleasant maybe, but under the surface he wasn't so sure.

"Then, of course, there's Johnston, my colleague. Dispassionately, I would describe him as fit, powerful, ruthless and, as you have observed, handy with a gun."

"Is that it?" asked Amanda. "It seems too few for so sophisticated an establishment."

"I think so. I've never seen nor heard them speak of anyone else."

Jack nodded again. "That's the only folks I saw."

"Anything else?" Harris asked.

Amanda had apparently heard enough. "Let's go." With her on point, Jack at the rear and Harris between them, all three set off toward the metalled road which led to the main island.

It was night now, but it wasn't fully dark, and a summer moon assisted the journey. Progress was still slow. There was no guarantee that danger would be deferred until they reached Main. Amanda was on full alert and at every unexplained sound stopped until satisfied it was safe to proceed. They weren't interrupted, and the journey to the connecting bridge passed uneventfully. At the bridgehead they stopped.

"Let me check it," Harris said. "This bridge has been shut for vehicles for a while and it's not in great condition."

Amanda nodded. "Very slowly, Captain."

Harris took this command literally. He fell to the ground and, on his hands and knees, began a slow crawl across the bridge. Amanda and her shotgun never left him.

Back at the head of the bridge, Jack lazily pushed and pulled on the solid metal top rail; the structure seemed robust enough. What was Harris doing and why was he taking so long?

Harris stopped at the far end of the bridge and then crawled back, studying something carefully. Eventually he returned holding a flat circular form.

"An anti-personnel mine connected to a trip wire. Crude but effective. That'll be Johnston's work. Not sure if he'd killed me, he thought he would take no chances."

"Can you set it up again and detonate it from a distance?" Amanda asked.

For a scientist who specialised in bomb-making, it was a very easy commission for him.

They crossed the bridge safely and waited as Harris went to work. In a few minutes he declared himself finished and he joined them, holding a wire in his hand. While he had been working, Amanda had wandered a little off the road and selected a suitable place of concealment behind a few rocks surrounded by high tussock grasses.

"Is it safe for you to detonate now?" she asked Harris and, receiving an answer in the affirmative, he did so. It wasn't a deafening blast, but on an island in the middle of the Atlantic it was loud enough. The next sound was of a door opening, and a few moments later the outline of a figure of a man descended the road to the bridge. He was very tall, too tall for Fay, so it was either Delap's taciturn brother or the treacherous Johnston.

The moon skipped past a cloud and lit up the man's face. Jack didn't recognise him, so it must be Delap.

He was armed with what looked like a short machine pistol, and he approached the bridge brandishing the gun in one hand and a torch in the other. He shone the powerful light onto the bridge and, presumably receiving no visual confirmation of what he expected to find, he inched forward and made a detailed examination.

He was evidently not satisfied, and he turned and slowly walked back from the bridge and began to spray torchlight around. A beam of light came across them once, and then a second time, whereupon Delap began to move towards them, still with the machine pistol extended. Ten yards from them he stopped and conducted another search. Then, with slow strides, he started walking towards them.

This time, the flashlight seemed to linger a little longer on them. The next movement was of the machine pistol rather than the torch: the weapon commenced a circular motion and, then it stopped, pointing in their general direction.

Jack tensed. He should do something. But Amanda's hand was on him, holding him back. Then Delap leapt backwards in a failed attempt to halt the two shotgun rounds she blasted into his chest.

With this indiscreet announcement of their arrival on Main, there was now no need for stealth. Amanda urged Jack and the limping Harris up the steep incline in front of them, eschewing the road, heading instead across rough, rocky ground.

At the top of the rise, they fell flat on the hard surface. Amanda knew what she was doing: the choice of ground was good. Through the grasses, they had clear views of each of four cottage outbuildings.

All of them were well lit and, as they watched, a door opened. From the building farthest away, two figures emerged, black silhouettes for a moment then gradually revealed.

Harris nudged Amanda. "That's Johnston and the girl, Delap."

Chapter 47

In the bath of light from the cottage, Jack could see that they were both also armed – Angela Delap with a machine pistol similar to that carried by her late brother, and Johnston with something that looked like an AK47. Both were about fifty yards away, and while Jack, Amanda and Harris had an edge in surprise, they were disadvantaged by the range. At this distance it would take a miracle shot from a Browning, and the shotguns were equally ineffective.

They waited in the hope that the two would come nearer but they didn't, and instead returned to the house, closing the door behind them.

Jack knew that if Amanda had been sure only the two were around, she would have ordered them forward, but both Fay and Samms were unaccounted for – and the other two cottages were also bathed in light.

Amanda whispered to them to wait while she scouted the nearest cottage and set off low, first across the scrub, then the road, before finally diving flat into a dark area beside the gable end of the first cottage. Jack lost sight of her then and imagined she was scouting round the back. Whatever she was doing, it didn't take long and he spied her, again squatting alongside the gable wall. She raised her hand. It could only have been a request for an all-clear signal.

Jack raised his hand in response. But their timing was bad. Luck had deserted them. Just as she embarked upon her return journey, the door of the furthest cottage burst open and Johnston emerged. He noticed the fleeing figure of Amanda instantly and the night sky was lit up by a burst of gunfire. She was only halfway returned and then either was hit or stumbled. Either way, she was now in a desperate position, made worse by the appearance of Angela Delap and her machine pistol.

Jack didn't have to think. He didn't want her to die. He grabbed the bag from Harris and located a grenade. He wished he had paid more attention earlier. He pulled frantically and a bit came off in his hand. He had no idea what he was doing so he stood and threw it in the general direction of Johnston. It landed about midway between Johnston and Delap, exploded, but did not knock either down. It did, however, cause a sufficient distraction to allow Amanda to get to her feet and sprint to comparative safety behind the cottage gable.

Jack wasn't finished, and he wasn't going backwards. He moved towards Johnston. Although he had saved Amanda, it was now looking like a poor decision; both Delap and Johnston were now focusing upon him.

Ahead was the only option, and as he didn't know how to use the shotgun, he presented the pistol to them. It wasn't really a fair fight, but from behind, and only just missing his left ear, a projectile whirred past and a second grenade dispersed its deadly shrapnel and killed Johnston where he stood.

Delap was still alive but fled to a gap between the cottages. Jack was still about ten yards away, firing the Browning randomly and ineffectively.

His gun clicked empty, but Amanda had now regrouped and had control of her gun. For the third time that night, he faced imminent death before a destructive blast from Amanda's shotgun ripped into Delap's back and she fell forward, dead.

Jack fell down himself at that point through fatigue and terror, and presently Harris limped across, carrying the canvas bag and

Johnston's automatic rifle. It was limp at his side, and as he approached Amanda, he handed it to her. "Take it if you want, but you should trust me now. I've just saved both your lives."

It was a fair enough point, but Amanda took the gun anyway. "I'm pretty sure the first two buildings are clear, but let's check out this one." She pointed to the former home of Delap and Johnston.

Chapter 48

On the lawns at the front of the main house, Cora Samms stood motionless. The deafening blasts from weapons and miscellaneous explosions had stopped now, and she waited for a situation report. She was calm and firm in her purpose but caught herself taking repeated drags of her cheroot. Her wait was a short one, for two puffs later she was joined by James Fay.

His features were impassive and his bearing as formal as ever. His voice was also calm and well-modulated, but Cora knew somehow that he was anxious. She expected bad news.

He did not disappoint. "We have armed intruders, ma'am. Two, maybe three."

"I understood that Captain Johnston had cleared the base."

"Yes, so he said, although he was uncertain about Harris. I cannot understand it." He sighed. "Johnston is dead, ma'am. I saw it myself."

Samms nodded. "Angela and Shaun?"

His eyes fell for a moment and his voice got as close to emotional as she had ever heard. "Angela is dead, ma'am. I don't know about Shaun. But I am not confident. He is not answering his radio."

It was a report about as close to unrecoverable tragedy as Samms had ever received. Angela and Shaun were like family to her. They had been with her since they were curly-haired children, running around together in the old country. She had loved them and now she had lost them. This blow, added to the loss of Ash at the hands of Hunt, was catastrophic.

Her voice didn't break as she said, "We have no time to mourn their loss, James. We must proceed."

He nodded.

"They are not important, nor are you or I. They may be dead, and I may be soon, but our people will live on. We must not fail them." Fay looked straight ahead at her as she continued. "Go James, go. You have all the company information, all the money. Go and use the money wisely. On behalf of our people. Individuals are not important – you are there to lead and to serve."

He bowed again. He had never disobeyed her in his life, yet he continued to stand still in front of her. He fell to his knees in front of her, kissed her hand, then slowly rose, looked at her once more, bowed deeply and, in a faltering voice, said, "Ma'am."

They parted, he powering his way down the metal road to the harbour while she returned to her house.

Chapter 49

Amanda, Jack and Harris found nothing in the first two cottages, then entered the cottage where Delap had been and immediately set about a detailed and rapid examination of what seemed a communications centre.

There were papers, charts and a radio, but they added little to the mission. Amanda seemed anxious that they had not cleared the area properly. Worse, Harris was now limping badly and, as Jack helped him to a nearby chair, considerable trails of blood followed them.

Harris fell heavily into the seat and Amanda moved across to him and re-examined his leg wound. She lifted his shirt and seemed to be examining another wound in his side. She didn't say anything, but Jack could see she was concerned; however, she confined her treatment to another bandage tightly applied.

This done, she drifted across the room and began a further review, starting with three computer screens.

Amanda beckoned Jack across and he gaped at the images. He moved to descend the stairs, but she held him back. "Wait a minute." She went back to Harris. He was clearly in pain, but alert.

"You okay?" He nodded with a bit of spirit. "We're going down these stairs, but you need to guard our flank." He nodded and she handed him an automatic rifle, which he cradled with familiarity.

This leap of faith taken, Amanda led Jack down the short flight of stairs. They led to a narrow corridor which was home to three closed doors. She approached each one tentatively, although none yielded to her touch. Jack eventually added some value by remembering a set of keys he had observed upstairs, and he quickly bound up and down, returning with them.

After only one abortive try, the key which fitted the end door was in place and she turned it, making a deafening click in the silence. "Stand behind me, gun out."

She levelled the shotgun and stood a pace back. With a sharp kick, the door yielded, and the inner scene revealed nothing more dangerous than what looked like a man sitting at the far end of the room, knees up supporting his head. At her violent intrusion, he looked up.

The man was about forty, and, despite his slightly sunken, bloodshot eyes, looked in good shape. For the first time in a while, Amanda gave someone a chance. "Armed police. Identify yourself."

The man was surprisingly composed, and his voice was low but strong. He looked up at her. "James Trent."

The shotgun was still levelled at the man. "I've been looking for you, Mr Trent."

He shrugged. "Miss Barratt?"

She nodded. "Now what are you doing here, Mr Trent?"

"They think I killed someone."

"Did you?"

He looked at her and raised his head in exhaustion. "No, I already told you that."

Police interrogations weren't what they used to be. Amanda seemed satisfied at this stage. "Are you injured?"

He shrugged again. "Not really, few bumps and bruises, no sleep for a day or so. Otherwise, okay."

"Can you stand up?"

"Yes." He made no attempt to do so.

"I'm in a hurry, Mr Trent."

He was a tall man, although he was stooping a little. He yawned and stretched until she gave him his next instruction. "Slowly, very slowly, take off all your clothes. Throw them in the corner."

If he was surprised, it did not show, and he completed a slow striptease, depositing his grubby jeans and various accessories where indicated. He was in very good shape indeed, save for a couple of angry-looking lacerations on his torso.

"Jack, search the clothes. Thoroughly."

It wasn't a great job, but someone had to do it. Jack moved across, and, gingerly at first, examined the filthy clothes closely. "Nothing."

"Okay, give him them back. Get dressed, Mr Trent, and hurry up."

He seemed to feel no degradation at this means of search. "What now?"

"You come with us. I'm not certain whether you're guilty of murder. For what it's worth, I don't think so, but I'm not sure. However, if you are not, I will not leave you to die in this locked room. You come with us, and you do what I say. If you do not, I'll kill you. This is an active Home Office operation. I am in command. Do you understand?"

Trent nodded briskly. "Yes," he said, and, the deal concluded, they all withdrew from the cell.

Amanda turned her attention to the middle door. "Open this door, please, Mr Trent." He unlocked it at the first attempt and looked at her for his next instruction.

Despite his recent partial acquittal, Trent had evidently not been completely cleared, and Amanda used him to lead through the door and into the unknown. "Open the door and go in."

He did so and they followed close behind. This cell was identical to the other, save that along one of the side walls there was a single bed. On the bed was a figure curled up in a foetal position.

Amanda pushed Trent deep within the cell. "Against the back wall, Mr Trent, and stand still."

He did so, and she turned her attention to the figure on the bed, gently sobbing. With the shotgun still pointing, she shook the figure roughly, moved a step back and introduced herself again. "Armed police. Up."

The gentle sobbing continued, but Amanda was apparently all out of hankies and sympathy. Instead, she pulled the figure off the bed. The woman fell roughly on the floor and Amanda prodded her again with the gun.

Another, more urgent prodding produced a result, as the figure revealed itself to be a woman who, in other circumstances, might have been considered attractive. Not more than early thirties, Jack reckoned. The long-legged woman got awkwardly to her feet. She half-staggered against Trent and he, more gently than Amanda, helped her to stand alongside, supporting her arm.

Amanda pointed her shotgun at the woman. "Identify yourself." Her voice was more sullen than emotional.

"L-Laura Gibson, Doctor Laura Gibson."

Amanda then asked the same questions as before and issued the same instruction, requesting that Trent turn to the wall as she disrobed.

Jack didn't face the wall and watched as Gibson threw her clothes defiantly in front of her until naked before them. He searched the clothes as diligently as before and threw them back, this time without looking at her.

Amanda apprised Gibson of the situation and then, in a similar choreographed move, the four withdrew from the cell, whereupon Amanda conducted the same well-rehearsed routine for clearing the last of the cells.

Because there were now three people in front of Jack, he could not immediately see what lay within when the door crashed open. However, it was immediately clear that something was out of order, for Laura Gibson let out an ear-piercing scream and collapsed sideways into the arms of Trent. When Amanda pushed them inside against the far wall, Jack at last gained a decent view.

There was no bed nor indeed any furniture in the cell. There was, however, an empty bottle of what looked like whisky standing forlornly in the far corner. The man who lay face up and spread-eagled in the centre of the room might have been drunk, but a large pool of thick, reddish congealing liquid around him and the very large hole in his head meant probably not. He would never recover from this hangover.

This development certainly shortened Amanda's investigations, and after a cursory further examination of the room, as well as an even shorter investigation of the prone figure, she ushered all four of them back up the stairs and back to the ground floor command centre where Harris, who seemed no worse, was in control.

"All clear here," he said. "Not a peep."

Amanda stood lost in thought while Jack encouraged Trent and Gibson to sit down, which they did. There was a kettle and a coffee-making machine, but when he went to the kettle, Amanda snapped, "There's no time, leave it."

He withdrew sullenly but perked up when he spotted another bottle of whisky sitting alongside a computer. He picked it up and took a slug before offering it around. Trent and Harris joined in. Amanda demurred.

"How are you, Captain Harris?"

"It's not great and it's getting worse. Hard to put weight on it now."

"Right, you stay here – we'll be back, God willing."

Harris nodded and took another slug of the whisky.

Unexpectedly, she turned her attention to Trent. "Captain James Trent, formerly of her Majesty's Special Air Service." So, she knew more than just his name.

Trent said nothing and she looked at him closely.

"If I could trust you, you might be useful to us. We seek to prevent the theft of sensitive items of government property. Items which, should they fall into the wrong hands, might have very serious consequences. To achieve this, we need to move now. You will have gathered that this is a highly dangerous operation. Tonight, some have already died."

Trent said nothing. To leave him alive guarded by the fast-fading Harris was effectively to free him. "Will you help us?" she asked.

Trent was silent for a moment and then inclined his head. "Yes. What do you want me to do?"

Amanda approached him and cleared a space on a nearby desk. Jack joined them and paid attention as, through crude diagrams, she explained the location of the house, the harbour and the aircraft hangars. "There are at least two hostiles unaccounted for." Here she let Jack describe Samms and Fay. "There may be others we do not know. Our priority is prevention of a shipment." She added chillingly, "Shoot only to kill."

Gibson, fingering her short, dark hair in an agitated fashion, asked, "What do I do?"

"You stay here, Doctor Gibson."

Jack wasn't sure whether this was the answer she sought, but she did not argue and asked another question. "What is it that has been stolen?"

"That's classified, Doctor Gibson." Amanda choked off a further exchange by beginning an examination of her weapons, adding magazines to her jacket pockets and carefully loading the automatic shotgun until it was full.

Jack also replaced the magazines in both of his Brownings.

"What do I get?" Trent asked.

This was an important question. Amanda looked at Jack questioningly.

So, she didn't have all the answers. He nodded to her.

She delved into the bag and threw Trent a pistol and, after a short pause, threw him magazines, which he caught.

It was clear that Trent knew what he was doing, and he checked out the gun carefully and then loaded it. This done, he stuffed it in his trousers and walked across towards Amanda. "Anything else?"

She moved aside and allowed him free access to the canvas bag.

He settled on an automatic assault rifle and a couple of grenades, which he slipped into his pockets. Amanda took the remaining grenades and moved back to the front door of the cottage.

She furtively looked outside and then to Harris. Almost tenderly, she put her hand on his shoulder.

Harris was fading fast, very fast, but with a brave voice he said, "Good luck."

She put her hand against the side of his head. "Thanks." She turned to her soldiers, Jack and Trent. "Let's go."

Chapter 50

The light of the night had not deteriorated further and the metalled road up to the house was easy to follow. All was quiet, and Amanda led them in a fast-moving column to the top of the hill.

The house was on the right and the airship and its hangars left, with the jetty beyond. An aircraft would be impossible to pursue and was the ideal means of escape, so they headed first for the dark forms of the hangars. The 400-yard walk between high crops was highly suitable for an ambush, but they arrived unmolested at the first of the open hangars.

It was darker inside than out, and there were numerous dangers in exploring the entire area. There was no need anyway; a further quarter of a mile away stood the silhouetted form of the Lear jet, dark and obviously not being prepared for take-off.

Amanda nudged her colleagues, and they walked briskly back to the end of the house, but before they arrived and only about a further hundred yards away, two figures came into view. A second later the duo split, and when the three of them arrived at the house's gable, they had disappeared almost out of sight, one headed to the harbour, the other towards the house.

There was no time now. "Jack – go to the house. It looks like Samms. We will head to the jetty."

The unmistakeable sound of a ship's engines starting floated through the summer night and Amanda and Trent broke into a sprint. They disappeared from view as they began their descent to the harbour.

Left alone for the first time, Jack felt an involuntary shiver run down his back. In terms of a systematic approach to storming a mansion, he was a novice. It was one thing following a professional like Amanda or Trent, but quite another to suddenly, and without even basic training, go solo. He fingered the Browning. There were several problems. Firstly, he was facing an unknown number in the house – it might be just Samms, but he could not be sure. Secondly, whoever was in the house undoubtedly knew the house better than him. And thirdly, he would be facing someone for whom the exercise was for a cause worth laying down their life for. He considered simply lying on the ground outside in wait, but that seemed cowardly.

It was also selfish. Whoever was in the house might leave via another exit, elude him and outflank Amanda and Trent. It was time to get on with his job. He hurried along the front of the house, jogging full-length past windows from which an assassin would have a straightforward shot, until he reached the front door.

This proved no barrier either, nor did it call for heroics. The door was unlocked and he moved through, leading with his gun, and scanned the inner reception area. Most of the house lights were full on but the hall was empty. This was all very easy thus far, but now his problems began. Up the stairs or through the closed doors on the ground floor? There were two doors either side of the central staircase. He had been through the one on the right, so he went left. With a sudden surge of adrenalin, he burst through the door, which led to a bland, unfurnished corridor which was home to numerous other closed doors.

It was an ideal scenario for any defender, but, in a fit of madness, he ignored that and ran past the doors, settling for a brave and foolish charge towards the single door at the corridor end. He crashed through the door, flashing the pistol in every direction. The room turned out to be a massive lounge, exquisitely furnished with broad bay windows, which would undoubtedly command stunning views. There was a low-lit fire which gave warmth to the room, and although the room was empty, it had only been recently vacated – the flickering light from the fire highlighted a slow-moving pall of cigarette smoke.

He had smelled that smoke before – from Samms' endless cheroots – and as the adrenalin faded, he started to use his brain. He knew where she would be. He left the lounge, and without exploring the perils of the other rooms, he returned to the hall. Passing the stairs, he burst into the sister corridor on the ground floor and entered the ornate medieval room in which he had recently dined. He made his way through the room and between the heavy tapestries.

This door he remembered, and also the location of the wall button. The door slowly opened to reveal the spiral ramp. The underground gallery was already lit. Jack slowed his pace as he descended. He knew what awaited.

Chapter 51

"Good evening, Mr McLeod. Have you come to sell me your picture?"

For some reason which he could not rationalise he said, "My name is Edwards, Jack Edwards."

She said nothing to that. She was standing some distance away, engaged in a review of one of her remaining masterpieces.

He walked towards her. As he did, his arm involuntarily fell, and when he arrived beside her, the gun was pointing at the floor. Why had that happened? He did not like her; every death had been her fault. He should shoot her on the spot. There was also a significant risk that she would shoot him, but something told him that she would not; not here.

Cora Samms was dressed elegantly, almost regally, with a silver black gown and her shoulders covered with a thin black shoulder wrap. Her black hair was set high off her face, and the few silver streaks visible perfectly highlighted her long diamond earrings.

"Do you care for Bacon?" she enquired.

Jack looked up at a study of the Screaming Pope. Automatically, he nodded.

"Unfortunately, this is not the final version. I'm afraid the Americans will not sell. Money does not always settle these things, as of course you know, Mr Edwards. Do you think Velasquez would have approved?"

"Of the brushwork and colour, or the message?"

"Yes, all of that."

Jack thought about it and said, "Well, yes, actually. To be copied after 350 years is pretty flattering. I think Velasquez would consider the work a little underdone but he might accept the message; it may be that Bacon's right about the state of the Roman Church."

"An interesting point of view, Mr Edwards. Are you a Romanist?"

"No, Church of Scotland."

"An interesting church, Mr Edwards." She did not elaborate.

She moved along half a dozen frames or so, with him pliantly following, and pointed at a fine portrait of an unknown nobleman. "As you say, Mr Edwards, brilliant colours and brushwork – a typical Velasquez portrait. I managed to get this from under the nose of the Prado."

Without thought to his mission, Jack appraised the master's work, but he remembered Amanda and Trent. He had to do something.

He cut short his art appreciation. "We have your man, captured him at the jetty. We've got the consignment. It's going nowhere."

She looked at him placidly through her grey eyes and said, "I do not think so, Mr Edwards."

And that seemed to be that. His bluff had been called and he had no Plan B.

In defiance of Amanda's shoot-to-kill policy, he decided to talk. At least he had her contained. He got straight to the point. "Why have you stolen these bombs?"

"Don't you know, Mr Edwards?"

He didn't feel confident in a second bluff. "Not exactly."

She seemed mildly amused in the face of this pathetic interrogation. "Obviously I cannot tell you this precisely, Mr Edwards, but you will remember, when you were my guest, that I once commented on those without a country."

He nodded.

"Well, I lead a people that currently have no country, and to get it back we need help. These bombs, as you call them, will do this."

"Do what? Kill millions?" He was angrier now but she was icy calm.

"Great causes require great sacrifices, Mr Edwards."

"And millions of others must make these sacrifices for your cause."

This seemed to sting her for the first time. "Mr Edwards, my ancestors were collecting art, practising social justice and tolerance and enlightening the world when your royal family were hunter-gathering in swamps. We are a great people and will be avenged and our leadership restored. I may not see it nor, indeed, will my nephew. He is dead, but he has been avenged."

An image of Hunt's shattered skull.

"So, please do not lecture me on causes and sacrifices."

He had run out of initiatives and looked at her standing proudly, every inch a Persian princess. She looked as if she had lived for centuries, and Jack could not compete with her passion and certainty.

The sound of fast-approaching footsteps brought him back to the present. They both looked round, she impassively and he astonished.

Dr Laura Gibson appeared, eyes blazing as she brandished an automatic rifle.

Chapter 52

Fay had had a five-minute start on Amanda and Trent, and they caught a short glance of his silhouetted figure on the boat, conducting some tasks in obvious preparation for embarkation. Unless they could rapidly close the distance, interception would be impossible.

They ran recklessly down the road in the dim light, each stride nearer Amanda hoping Fay would delay. They had a slight advantage as he was not looking in their direction.

Their luck ran out at about a hundred yards away, though, as Fay turned to untether the ship. As he did so, he looked back. A second later they had to dive to the ground to escape a wall of automatic fire which traced in their general direction. They split either side of the road. Amanda's shotgun was no use, but Trent returned fire from across the road with the automatic.

The fire from the boat seemed stronger than the return, but having created two targets, Amanda was now free to close in on the boat. Her progress was slow, however, and she soon halted as there was no cover.

The firefight continued, which gave her hope, but when a succession of hand-launched grenades exploded in a blaze of light very near to Trent's last-known position, prospects took a turn for the worse.

Fire was coming only one way now and Fay seemed to have

declared victory. He threw down his weapon and disappeared from view, back into the boat.

Amanda had inched to within fifty yards now, but the throaty roars from the boat's engine were increasingly urgent. She was too far away still, but in frustration she discharged the shotgun. As expected, this achieved nothing, so she threw down the gun, sprinted and delved into her pockets. Now she was, agonisingly, only ten or so paces from the boat. Its gears engaged, and it started to move.

Amanda removed the pin and launched a grenade. It was a straight, true and well-thrown pitch, but before it landed, the boat shot forward, and the resultant explosion was lost in the tumult in the water of the boat's wake.

A miss of five yards might have condemned millions to their death. Despite missing the boat, Amanda turned tail and ran like the wind. Trent was alive and was sitting on the road. Although his voice was strong and his denials convincing, it seemed likely that he was badly hurt. There was no time to investigate further. She had to leave him, and urged her tired limbs and bursting lungs forward until she regained the front lawns of the house.

The fate of millions might have been at risk, but her humanity was based on a bottom-up approach and started with individuals. She had left Trent sitting but would return for him. Right now, she was in search of Jack.

Chapter 53

Jack's surprise at Laura Gibson's arrival had gone now, replaced by astonishment at her transformation from a sobbing innocent to what now seemed a woman of determination and purpose.

She was not looking at Jack, and indeed seemed oblivious to his presence. Her total focus, via fiery eyes, was on Cora Samms, a focus which she did not relinquish while she raised the assault rifle into a parallel position.

Samms was in deadly peril, but Jack could discern no change in her bearing. He had no idea what to do, so he did nothing as the bizarre drama played out in front of him. Gibson's voice had also changed. While it was charged with emotion, it was strong with passion and determination. She halted about four paces from Samms and they regarded each other silently for an age.

Gibson broke the silence and in a low steady voice said, "You bitch. You ugly bitch. Who do you think you are?"

No answer came to this rhetorical question and Gibson, her eyes wild, continued, "I've listened to you talk, talking about your causes. What gives you the right? Who cares about your causes? Certainly not your nephew. He didn't care about causes – just where to get his next line of coke. A worthless piece of trash, a sponger, a waste of space. That's all he was."

Samms just looked at her, and Gibson finished her story with a smile of triumph.

"So why should I feel bad about ending it for him? After all, that's what you do with a dying dog – put it out of its misery."

She stared hard at Samms again as if waiting for a response, but again nothing came back. "He died on his knees – I put a skewer through his neck. It went in – so easily. He fell amongst bags of rubbish, which," she reflected matter-of-factly, "was, all in all, pretty appropriate."

Nothing could stop her now. "And do you know why? Of course you don't. Your prince, if that's what he was, well, he found out something about a man, a man I loved. Do you know what love is, you desiccated bitch?"

She gave a hollow laugh. "Of course, you don't. Your prince, he came to me and said he would ruin him if he didn't pay. Not just that – he wanted me … to have me too. So, I killed him."

Her voice softened. "He was a good man, the man I loved." She paused again and then, with a new and unmatched venom, said, "And you killed him. He's lying down there in one of your cells with his brains blown out. You weren't even clever enough to work out who had killed your little boy."

Samms looked majestic in the face of this assault, Gibson utterly determined. And Jack felt frozen. He looked first at Samms and then at Gibson, the latter now silent and taking a step backwards while positioning the assault rifle with obvious purpose. He watched for a few seconds that felt like hours, unable to settle on any course before, without warning, Gibson was reduced to silence, courtesy of a bullet through her brain from a silver pistol held by the extended hand of Cora Samms.

Majesty had prevailed, and Samms' expression was triumphant. And it didn't change when she, slowly and elegantly, crumpled forward as Amanda's bullets hit her hard and full in the chest.

Jack's brain was exploding. Should he shoot himself to somehow complete the final act of this tragedy?

He was pulled to his senses by Amanda, who grabbed him roughly around the neck and drew him towards her, holding him very tight.

Life was preferable to death – that much he was sure of.

Chapter 54

Jack held Amanda tightly for another moment, then disengaged as she issued further instructions. They ran back down the hill to the cottage headquarters. Harris's shirt was soaking with fresh red blood. He looked dead – and he was. Jack cursed while Amanda urgently fiddled with a radio receiver, which crackled incoherently despite her promptings.

She swore like a crude tradesman appraising a botched job. Jack located a bottle of whisky while she worked and moved across to join her when the crackling receded and took form in a clear, clipped English voice.

"Her Majesty's Ship George," the voice said. "British destroyer cruising in the North Atlantic. Please do not use this frequency. Over."

Amanda had a patchy record of following orders and she was having a bad day. She keyed into the frequency again. "Amanda Barratt, Home Office, on the Isles of Grace. Please put on your captain." She then muttered a lot of mumbo jumbo codes which, Jack imagined, were aimed at establishing her bona fides.

The next voice that came through represented modest progress. "Captain Butler, HMS George. Good evening, Miss Barratt. What can I do for you? Over."

She explained that Fay's boat must be intercepted.

"We are aware of the movements of this vessel, Miss Barratt. It is now in contact with another vessel, and I regret that both are in international waters, so interception is impossible."

Amanda swore. "Captain Butler, if you are not empowered, I demand that you refer this request. Over."

There was a short pause then another voice came through. This voice did not have a name, only a nickname. It was double Dutch to Jack, but it must have meant something to Amanda, for she stood a little taller and addressed the voice as "Sir"

A short exchange then followed and Amanda's request, despite having achieved her requested escalation, remained denied.

The voice had a few requests of its own. "Please secure the area and await collection. Miss Barratt, we estimate our arrival as thirty minutes. Have you any wounded?"

"One," she said.

The voice went on. "Miss Barratt, could you do me the courtesy of advising me on the whereabouts of our Colonel Michael Shaw – we seem to have mislaid him."

Amanda's lips twitched. "I may be able to assist when picked up, sir."

He let this go with a laugh. "Over and out."

Suddenly Jack was very, very tired; he slumped to his knees and then to the floor.

Amanda wasn't finished. "Wait here. I'll be back in a few minutes. Keep alert."

Those minutes passed and Jack had just summoned enough energy to return to the whisky bottle when, from outside, there was the unmistakeable sound of approaching footsteps.

Jack drew his gun wearily, but re-holstered it when Amanda burst in with Trent, who looked about as bad as most of the others Jack had seen that night, and they had all been dead.

An urgent emergency examination revealed a bad-looking, but not life-threatening shoulder wound, either from a bullet or a shard of grenade. Amanda took the whisky bottle from Jack and gave it to Trent. He flopped in a chair and took several sloppy slugs.

Amanda joined Jack on the floor and cradled his head in her arms as they waited.

Sick at heart and utterly exhausted, neither Jack, Amanda nor Trent reacted quickly enough to further sounds from outside the cottage, and they were beaten and unprepared when a four-strong squad of special forces soldiers, without knocking, crashed into the cottage.

They ordered the exhausted trio to throw their visible weapons into the centre of the room.

One of the soldiers then spoke. "Are you Miss Barratt?"

Amanda nodded.

"The Director's compliments, ma'am. He will join you presently."

"Thank you, Captain," she ventured.

"Major, ma'am," he corrected her respectfully. "Would you like a cup of coffee, ma'am?"

It was all pretty civilised, and the balaclava-wearing major made coffee and handed one to each of them. Jack indicated the bottle of whisky on the table and the major waited on each of them, flavouring the hot, black coffee to order.

Chapter 55

No one had the energy for speech so they sat in silence, drinking coffee, until a man without a balaclava entered and the major and his squad stood to attention.

The man wore combat fatigues, boots and a thick cream ribbed cardigan. He was about sixty but didn't look it, for he was well preserved, still had a full head of hair and was tall, lean and powerful.

He looked across to Amanda. "Hello, Amanda."

She muttered a reciprocal greeting.

"You have an injured man," he said, looking at Trent.

"Captain James Trent, formerly of Her Majesty's Special Forces."

The Director nodded and directed the major, who detailed two of his troops. They helped Trent to his feet, then headed off with the invalid.

This done, he said to Amanda, "And this is Mr Jack Edwards, not of HM Forces?"

"Yes, but temporarily seconded to the Home Office, sir."

He nodded and addressed the major. "I think we are fine here. I suggest you return and help co-ordinate. The boat will be loaded in about thirty minutes, but hurry them up."

The major nodded and he and his remaining trooper departed. The Director walked across and picked up a coffee cup, then filled it with whisky. He pulled out a chair from behind a desk and pushed it to the middle of the room, sitting above them as they remained seated on the floor.

"Well, Miss Barratt, this is all a bit of a mess."

It was impossible to disagree; by Jack's rough calculations nine were dead, with four weapons of mass destruction stolen. If this wasn't a mess, it was hard to imagine what would be.

The Director did not develop his treatise. "Mr Edwards has signed the Official Secrets Act?"

Bureaucracy, even at a time like this.

Amanda nodded, and with this reassurance he went on with confidence. "Yes, all very unfortunate. As I see things, Captain Johnston seems to have gone mad. A sudden brainstorm." He shook his head. "Well, there was always that risk in a place like this." He cheered up. "Still, if we tidy things up, I think we can achieve containment."

This all seemed clear enough to the Director, but Jack had questions. He had signed the Official Secrets Act, so he was entitled to speak, surely? "Have you intercepted the boat?"

The Director seemed rueful. "Alas no. Really doesn't do, boarding foreign vessels in international waters."

Jack agreed with the rule of maritime law but surely grounds existed for a bending of the rules. "Do you know what you've lost?"

It was a stupid question to Britain's top spy.

"Well, Mr Edwards, it's not clear that we've lost anything. It seems that there's been a fire in the facility and nearly all the records have been lost. However, I feel sure that when we check we'll be able to account for everything. All in all, we've been pretty lucky.

"Still, if we have lost any devices, we will know where they are headed and" – he took a draught of whisky – "there are so many struggles in the world. So hard to separate right from wrong. One man's terrorist's another man's freedom fighter, that sort of thing."

He broke off from further philosophical thoughts. "Besides which, all the devices have integrated, unremovable tracking devices, and should they find their way to the wrong place, we can remotely disable them."

"And if they are in the right place?" Jack enquired.

The Director smiled benevolently. "Actually, the technology, while new to the rest of the world is, to us, several generations old. Brilliant man, Captain Johnston. So, you see, even if they were to fall into the wrong hands, foreign powers wouldn't learn much."

The Director then arrived at what seemed to Jack a breathtaking closing summary. "Really, our facility has been exceptionally successful. Pity about Johnston."

The Director took another long mouthful of whisky, his thoughts on the matter apparently exhausted. He drained his mug, stood up and replenished it. "Now, Amanda, if Mr Edwards has no more questions, perhaps he could make his way down to the harbour. I would like to have a word with you alone."

Jack was out of questions and he looked at Amanda, who nodded. He picked up the canvas bag, left the cottage and headed for the jetty. As he slowly walked up the road to the main house, it became obvious that a significant number of soldiers must have landed for there were voices calling from everywhere, presumably engaged in what the Director had dubbed "tidying up"

Jack passed two troopers carrying a body, and the size and form of it suggested that it might have been Samms. They were heading away from the house and away from the harbour. Only a pauper's grave lay ahead for Cora Samms, and he shuddered at the thought. When he gained the top of the road, a single soldier stood like a traffic policeman, directing men left and right. In the distance the Lear jet was being powered up.

Obviously, the moveable assets were faring better than the dead, and his mind moved on to the fate of Samms' art collection. The directing soldier looked a bit like the one he had seen before. "Major?"

"Yes, Mr Edwards?" the major replied.

"Could I go into the house? Have a last look at the artworks?"

He considered for a moment. "Ten minutes, Mr Edwards."

At this, Jack wasted no time and was soon back in the floodlit gallery. This was also teeming with soldiers who, with some assistants dressed in civilian clothes, were taking down and carefully packing the remaining masterpieces.

At his approach, the leader of this heist listened in to a walkie-talkie and then met him. "Afraid we'll have to work on, Mr Edwards. Have a look around, but I'd be grateful if you don't get in the way."

The liquidators of Cora Samms' estate proved to be working efficiently and, after Jack had stopped three times to admire a picture only for it to be removed from the wall, he gave up. The total value had to amount to over a billion pounds, and its artistic content close to priceless, but he doubted whether HM Government would have much interest in artistic merit.

Jack shuffled back out of the house. He doubted whether they would be sold. Probably not. A darker fate awaited the works – confinement sine die at 170 Brighton Road, the Government Surplus Unit.

He couldn't feel sorry for Samms, but he felt sorry for the collection. He turned the knob on the front door but, as he did so, he halted as a wild thought came to him.

The hall and rest of the house was quiet and without soldiers. On a whim, he turned around and bounded up the central stairs two at a time. He flicked on a light, which revealed the familiar scene of the bedroom he had stayed in earlier that week.

He moved quickly past admirable works by Degas, Monet and Dix before stopping and admiring a medium-sized oil by Edward Hopper. Hopper was an artist who specialised in portraying, with simple clarity, the loneliness of the human race. The oil was good: a typical example. A middle-aged man standing in the middle of a brilliant yellow mid-western field, his simple white timber house in the distance. Alone, like Samms. Maybe even like Jack.

With a determined rush of blood, he lifted it from the wall, stuffed it into the canvas bag and, with a thrill, raced back down the stairs, left the house and made his way to the jetty. There were only three boats in harbour now: Samms' yacht alongside a crude metal affair which looked like it had delivered the soldiers, and the third a comfortable-looking medium-sized supply boat. He walked to the last and sat on the jetty beside it, smoking a cigarette.

He was attended by another military figure who approached him jauntily. "Off in five minutes, Mr Edwards. The Director and Miss Barratt will be here presently."

Presently was about two minutes. He threw down his cigarette and stood up.

"Are you ready, Mr Edwards?" the Director asked.

"Yes." He put his arm around Amanda and helped her onto the boat.

The Director was evidently not joining them at this stage.

Suddenly Jack had an attack of guilt and he jumped back off the boat. Opening the bag, he said, "I have taken a souvenir from one of the guest bedrooms."

There was enough light from the ship to illuminate the picture. "Hopper," the Director said appreciatively. "As I recall, our records do not include this Hopper in the Samms' collection." He replaced the oil in the bag. "Have a good trip, Mr Edwards."

Chapter 56

Amanda met Peter in her office, and after a short conference, they left for Marylebone police headquarters.

Bradley's cold was better and he was now working hard on a sore back. He moved gingerly and explained why he was unable to rise.

Amanda sat down. "Well, Danny, I've got an update on your murder."

Bradley grimaced and rubbed his back. "Good, I don't think we are much further on."

"Oh, I wouldn't say that. In fact, you've been ahead of me the whole way."

Bradley apparently forgot about his back for a moment and he leant forward.

"Anyway, don't worry,' Amanda said. 'I think we can get you a quick result. There were three suspects. You know them all. Jimmy Trent, Ash's business partner. I've been able to clear him. Doctor Jasper Hunt – I was also able to clear him as well, but unfortunately he got killed before I was able to tell him about his good fortune."

Bradley was sitting erect and far back in his seat now.

"And the third suspect. That was Doctor Laura Gibson." She swallowed down the image of that night on the island. "Well, it seems she was guilty, but don't worry: she got shot and killed as well. So, all in all a neat job, and not too much paperwork."

Bradley stared at her.

"Oh, I have some of the documentation here." She turned to Peter, who handed her the envelope, and she sprayed four A4 photographs across Bradley's desk.

He didn't scan them; he looked at each of the photographs for a long time.

"The big guy there is a Mr Fay," Amanda said. "Well, he's the man who abducted the three of them and administered this rough justice. His information was spot on. He knew everything we did. Not before we did, but just a little after us. He certainly acted quicker than us."

She stopped and Bradley looked up. He looked genuinely ill now. Amanda got up. "Come on, Danny. It's time."

He got up slowly and followed them out of his office.

A few paces on he stopped at a desk and stood up tall. With a strong resigned voice, he said, "Jason Rose, I'm arresting you on suspicion of conspiracy to murder. You do not have to say anything but what you do say may be used against you in evidence."

Chapter 57

Thirty-six hours after leaving the Isles of Grace, Jack Edwards awoke from a deep sleep. Glancing through tired eyes, he saw that the clock indicated eleven, and through the open window of his hotel room the persistent distant roar of traffic was reassuring.

Amanda wasn't sitting on his bed today, so he struggled to his feet and swayed a little as he undertook the short walk to the shower. Any other day his reflection in the honest mirror would have concerned him, but today, as the hot water danced off his body, he had no complaints.

He was fortunate to be alive. Only three of them had made it off the island. Ten were dead, and he inexplicably started to mourn them by singing a current popular song in an enthusiastic but tuneless blast. It wasn't that he felt nothing for the dead, but the overwhelming gratitude that he had been spared selfishly dominated his thoughts. Spared for what?

He bounded out of the shower and dressed quickly. This done, he left the hotel and a short, uneventful taxi ride took him to the auction house. His timing was good.

The well-clipped tones of the auctioneer announced Lot 85 and Jack shuffled around, eyeing a few inferior pieces before stopping for a final appraisal of the JD Fergusson. Something about it seemed inexplicably and subtly different, but he was still satisfied. The salesman behind the desk ran through ten more lots, pretending to have sold them all by bidding up to the reserve, and then it was Lot 96.

Jack always liked to bid in person for a work. Even although he never now risked short-term financial disaster with a bid, it had never lost its thrill. Perhaps it was the public nature of the event, or perhaps the thrill of declaring his wealth, but no matter, it was still fun.

The slick auctioneer mumbled a few platitudes about the artist and the work. Apparently, it was an excellent example which, in the case of this lot, was true.

Despite this glowing build-up, he kicked off well under the low estimate, and Jack and the auctioneer swapped numbers until, at £220,000, Jack had cleared the book. This would have been a very good price, but his luck did not hold, and two annoying interventions from a telephone cost him an extra £60,000.

Overall, when the exorbitant buyer's premium – the house percentage – was added, Jack was declared the new owner of the work at the bargain price of £335,000. It was quite a high price, but it was quite a good painting and he could afford it.

He paid up and took the oil with him. He left the auction house, successfully hailed a taxi, and carefully loaded himself and the Fergusson inside.

Once back at his room in the Grange, he carefully placed the Fergusson on a handy supporting ledge and, after delving into the canvas bag, he lifted out the Hopper and placed it alongside. Jack loved JD Fergusson's work, but the Hopper was better – more original, less derivative and more colourful than even the best Scottish colourist could manage.

He turned to the Hopper and now all he could see were events on the island. Passion and certainty, blood and death. He shuddered. Then he was furious at the complicity and brigandry of both the Samms' and HM Government's gangs, but it was all too much to rationalise. What he could understand was that it was over, at least for now.

Who had won the game was less certain. Samms and most of her staff were dead, but Fay would surely commit himself to Samms and her cause for as long as it took. The British Government had cleared artworks north of a billion pounds and had abetted a clear, albeit covert, breach of the strictest international treaties.

Despite the Director's casual confidence, the risks to come were uncertain. However, if the ultimate result of the match between Samms and MI6 could not be called, there were certainly some losers. Not the dead – they were beyond suffering – but millions of people going about ordinary daily life unaware that, at any moment, destruction might be visited on them.

The other loser was, as ever, the truth, whatever it was.

He had a part in this. Maybe he could pretend to himself that his role had been noble, to try to save a man and perhaps prevent a tragedy. It was the lie you told yourself that mattered, and, for the sake of his sanity, Jack was hanging on to this one like a limpet.

He moved his gaze back to the Fergusson oil painting, and, with a blinding flash of clarity, understood why, despite its shortcomings, he preferred it. It wasn't the Hopper's fault, but it had been bought with blood, and there might be more, much more to come. He would never be able to view it, ever, on its own merits.

His stomach rumbled loudly. He had not eaten properly for days and he figured he should give it a go. He made his way into the thinly patronised restaurant in the Grange, sat down and reviewed the lunch menu.

After twice sending away a persistent waiter, he finally gave his order. "A large Jack Daniel's, please. No food."

This order was prepared quickly, and, on its receipt, he rose from the dining chair and went out through the French windows which led to the small overgrown garden. He took a seat on an uncomfortable but solid garden chair, lit a cigarette and took a long slug of the bourbon. It exploded angrily against his empty stomach, but today it didn't hurt. Today he was immune to pain.

Parthian Shot
by
Adam Parish

Book 2 of the
Jack Edwards and Amanda Barratt
Mystery Series

Also by Adam Parish
The Quartermaster (1)
Loose Ends (3)

To sign up for offers, updates
and find out more about Adam Parish
visit our website www.adam-parish.com

Printed in Great Britain
by Amazon

82434701R00123